Bourbon & Boss

Annie Rae

ISBN: 978-1-7370057-3-5

ASIN: B0BZK51GGC

Cover design by: Matador Designs

Printed in the United States of America

To my Ride or Die,

I always knew you were one of a kind, but this year has been like
no other.

Couples vow in sick and health, but the reality is not all hearts and
flowers. It's pain and surgeries, taking the
brunt of house work and carpools, groceries, and cooking.

You did all that. And you did it with love. Still encouraging me and
supporting me with my work.
Keeping me laughing and giving me those giant bear hugs that
make the sun shine every day.

I love you so much! I could never do this thing called life without
you.

Chapter One

Bree

*B*om. *Bom. Bom. Bom. Bom. Bom. Boda badom.*

London's Calling drowns out the silence in the back kitchen. Electric guitars and keyboard strumming over the bass drum in my headphones. The perfect punk beat to knead the dough under my palms. My hips tick. My toes dancing inside my slide-ons to one of my favorite bands.

Tucker shits a brick every time he sees these shoes in the kitchen, but what he doesn't know won't hurt him. That's part of why I love these off hours.

Anytime I can't sleep, I blast rock music or oldies, and work out my frustration on a new pastry. This morning, I've perfected the thin phyllo dough under my roller. There's a stainless-steel bowl of pumpkin cream cheese filling waiting in the fridge. After a few more passes of the rolling pin, I'll cut the dough into strips, and they should be ready for a butter brush.

This one's going to be amazing. Picture-perfect pumpkin pastries. Fancy enough for *Two-Fourteen*. Delicious enough for the fall festivals, this town goes gaga over. Surprisingly, these crazy holiday gigs have grown on me in the last year. Despite the incessant gossiping, people are relatively welcoming. And so far, I've steered clear of the match-making little biddies and small town drama.

Could be because you never get your tits out of the kitchen.

Don't really care, though. Insomnia contributed to the Rolodex of desserts in my head. Now, I finally have a place to use them.

It helps to have a boss nice enough to open his kitchen to his motley crew kitchen staff. When the darkness of my apartment becomes too much, I escape here. Dance beats energize my hands—and my thoughts—and I create a new masterpiece. Even if most of the time I'd prefer to lick the sweet creams off his body.

No. Nope. Not happening. I will not think about Tucker tonight.

It's bad enough that I can't stop myself from staring during service. I can't let that sexy smile slip into my head and distract when he's not even here.

Just because the man is hot as sin, doesn't mean he gets to live in my head rent free 24/7. That gregarious personality drives me up the freaking wall. Not that I should complain when he gave me a key to come and go as I please. Some nights, dreams make sleeping impossible. Years of hopping from one crappy foster home to the next took its toll. Tucker knows this unfortunately... Blame one unfortunate night of doubling shift drinks and the fact that tequila loosens my tongue.

Only, the past few months, my dreams have been less nightmare level and more of a climb-my-freaking-boss-like-a-mountain type.

Shaking my head, I bury those delusional thoughts in the trash where they belong. Dance-walking to the fridge and back helps. It's easier to feel like a loon than give into the idiotic urges Tucker brings out in me.

With the frigid bowl tucked in my arm, and slightly more re-solve, I belt out the chorus of my favorite song while spooning pumpkin in a neat little ball at the bottom of each dough strip. My hips wiggle back and forth, dorkifying my prep process. Thank all the nonstick in Williams Sonoma that no one is here to see it.

Laughing, I fold the lengths of dough into little triangles, already giddy for the golden-brown fall treats. A sense of calm washes over me as the last buttered pastry hits the baking sheet until a tap on my shoulder startles the bejeezus out of me. I duck my head, shrinking and somehow jumping at the same time. My elbow flies back, lightning quick, hitting a painfully hard wall of muscle.

"Shit!" Ripping an earbud from my ear, I toss it to the counter, flipping one-eighty, only to stare into the glowing hazel eyes I escaped in my dream.

"Woah, woah. Easy, kid..."

"Tucker—Chef—what are you doing here?"

"I own the place. What's your excuse?" A panty-melting smile lights up that too-handsome-for-my-own-good face, taking some of the sting off the snark.

"Couldn't sleep," I say, focusing on glazing my turnovers for the oven. One hundred percent not noticing the sexy layer of dusky blond stubble Chef showed up with instead of his standard, clean shave.

His head peers over my shoulder. "Hmm, cinnamon."

An electric current zings down my spine from his proximity, my heart rate ticking up until my cheeks burn and I have to duck away with my tray of goodies. Away from that intoxicating smell that hovers somewhere between leather and cedar and wood-fired grill.

How the man smells like a piece of smoked meat and perfectly clean at the same time, I don't know. It's one of my many frustrations. After a long night in the kitchen, I smell like raw flour and a hefty dose of sweat. While the chef—a man I shouldn't touch with a ten-foot pole—walks around smelling like a high-end steakhouse, all rich sauces and buttered herbs. It's freaking unfair!

With the turnovers in the oven, and nothing to distract my hands, I wipe down the counter, keeping three feet of stainless steel between us. Things have been a little testy in the kitchen these past few months, tension building whenever we're alone in the same room.

"It's a little early for the head chef. Aren't you working tonight?" The question snaps out harsher than I intend, and Tucker straightens, his back stiffening at the reminder of our roles.

"Aren't you?" Chef's eyes shutter back into stiff restaurant owner. Gone is the laid back, friendly coworker. This is exactly why I shouldn't think of Tucker as anything other than... boss. My big mouth guarantees trouble as soon as I forget our roles.

Right now, the boss is staring, waiting for a response as I tidy my space. I should get out of here. Searching Pinterest for recipe ideas is better than sticking my foot in my mouth. But why did he have to invade my morning?

I snatch my apron from my neck, hanging it on the hook by my station. "I am working tonight, and I will be on time. Don't worry. But I'd rather not spend hours staring at my ceiling. Figured I'd practice a few recipes, instead."

His eyes soften, and he angles his head at the oven. "What are you working on?"

"Pumpkin turnovers for the Taste of Kissing Springs."

"Ugh... Don't remind me."

"You're still doing a booth, right?"

"Yeah... I'm doing a booth. Smith is doing a booth. The catering company has been so goddamn crazed that we need a whole separate rig for him. Double the staff. Double the samples." He throws his hands up, running those long fingers through his unruly hair. "So many freaking weddings. So many appointments." His disgruntled response surprises me.

I don't like the lines drawing his brows together. It seems wrong for Chef's face to pinch with stress. A damn shame for our typically happy boss. "Damn love-obsessed town. Is it finally getting to you?"

My chest tightens at the thought of all these happy couples bombarding our town since the new mayor took over. The Romance Capital of the Sound... Barf. Bachelorette parties. Showers. Engagement parties. Weddings are a booming industry. It's lovey-dovey all over the whole damn town.

"Good for business," he says, eyeing me from across the table. "You're presenting recipes at the festival, right?"

"That's the plan. Feed the obsession."

"Literally." Tucker smirks, his gaze smoldering hotter than the pan in the oven. Sometimes I think Chef gets off on our sparring, the back-and-forth excitement. At least the ones in private. I bite my tongue in front of the staff out of respect.

Chef hired me on boasted skill and service by fire. I'm grateful for his trust, considering I showed up with a carload of belongings and forty dollars in my account.

Sweat trickles down the back of my neck remembering that time. "Do you need me out of the kitchen?"

"What? No!" Tucker glances at his watch, looking flustered.

Shrugging, I grab my apron, deciding against going home in favor of prepping tonight's pão de queijo. My hands need to stay busy, and I've been craving the Brazilian cheesy bread since I saw a commercial for a steakhouse in Lexington. Since I'll never have time to get there—or the money—that obsessive bread is on the list to make my own damn myself.

That Two-Fourteen allows me freedom to experiment is a huge plus.

Worth dealing with the walking sex-on-a-stick in relaxed-fit jeans watching me work. The worn to perfection kind. Not the trendy, machine-torn and bleached to within an inch of their life, kind. When he's not in chef's pants, like in these early morning hours, the boss wears these that seem velvet to the touch and cup a spectacular ass, which I have no business ogling.

Only, the more mornings Tucker finds me in his kitchen, the louder the little devil on my shoulder screams to be bad. The wee morning hours, before the sun peaks over the treetops, are freeing. And freeing with my boss is bad... Very bad.

Tucker leans his elbows on the countertop and my heart rate spikes. His rich scent threatens to overpower this morning's pastry, whose aroma is already making my mouth water after only a few minutes baking.

"Anything you need for service?" Chef asks, eyeing the ingredients spread between us.

I glance at my flour covered hands. "Nah... I pretty much got it. Although, I'll leave you the name of a Savarin cheese I'd love to add to next week's order. The distillery's having their employee appreciation party in a few weeks, right?"

His eyes widen. "Yeah. Thanks for remembering."

Instead of taking offense, I wave off his thanks and focus on the dessert pairings I've mapped in my head. I dart to the walk in for my cold ingredients, but when I come back to the table, Tucker is still lingering, watching as I mix milk, olive oil, and water. His spaced-out gaze is nothing unusual lately, however Tucker fixating as I stir two beaten eggs into my batter worries me.

"You gonna help or twiddle thumbs?" *Shit!* That's not what I meant to say. Embarrassment crawls up my spine, and I bite the back of my tongue when Tucker flushes. *Damn my smart-ass mouth.* "I mean, uh, is there something bothering you, Chef?"

Being the mature one, Tucker handles my mouth malfunction with a knowing smile, those dark amber eyes sparkling with kindness. His irises remind me of that goo at the end of the old man's cane in Jurassic Park. Gross in film. Completely mesmerizing in person. A fire of gold surrounded with fine lines that crinkle when he smiles, set out by a perpetual tan—even in Kentucky winter—that only looks hotter against the salt-and-pepper streaking the slightly shaggy hair at his temples.

"You know… I've got a mess of breakfast to prep to do, but I'm a willing guinea pig whenever you need a taster." He winks, and I want to slap the grin right off his face. Being so controlled while I'm so frazzled is damn annoying. My panties burn to ash whenever the man's around, and he just smiles as if nothing bothers him. Not a crazy service. Not getting in the weeds. Certainly not me.

We've done this dance all year. Late nights in the kitchen blur lines quicker than a Paper Mate eraser. Innuendos. Flirty banter that pushes right to the edge before we're interrupted—saved—by Mark or Vincent, sometimes Kelsey needing Chef in the front of the house.

Unaware of my errant train of thought, Chef moves to his station, pulling out the clean aluminum pans he uses for the VFW. At some point during the week, they end up cleaned and returned for the next meal. Few people know or acknowledge his donation. And he works without drawing attention to the effort he puts into preparations. It just is.

That freaking, unassuming generosity just makes his ass hotter. Infuriating, because as far as I can tell, Chef only sees me as the pink hair kid who's good with a piping bag. Good enough for an innocent flirtation, but the man probably thinks I'm too immature for the freaking romp in the hay I need. Or that I'd turn into a stage-five clinger.

Silence descends as we set to work. Feet apart, but it feels like worlds as I watch Chef chop and marinate. It's been too damn long since I had a non-battery-powered orgasm. I'm not some innocent flower. Life is hard. *Hell! Life fucking sucks sometimes.*

For months, I've fought the urge to make a move on Tucker, getting too turned up by riling him up. But I can't. I won't risk this job for a quick romp in the kitchen. No matter how long the dry spell.

Or how lickable the boss.

Chapter Two

Tucker

My eyes burn staring at the front door of the VFW building. Usually, this place is my third home. A safe space for guys like me.

This morning, my brain is solidly back in my kitchen with a spitfire who'd slap me in the face if she knew what I wanted to do with her on that prep counter.

Months of denying how that smart mouth challenges my common sense is wearing on me. Telling myself I should stay away from employees. I have rules. So why does this one turns all my expectations, all my priorities, on their head?

Last night was another sleepless night. One of many since I hired the pastry nymph.

"Fuck!" I slam my palm against the steering wheel, flexing my fingers when the knuckles go numb.

Hiring Bree was a brilliant business decision for Two-Fourteen... the woman's sweet game is an orgasm for the mouth. The problem is, wanting to give her a goddamn toe-curling, back-scratching orgasm in real life.

I can't.

Tap, tap, tap.

"Shit!"

Frustrated to be caught daydreaming, I snatch my key from the ignition and open my car door to Ben. The old staff sergeant runs the entire veterans' operation across our county. He's the go-to man, knowledgeable about everything from paperwork to discharges, the best facilities and doctors to heal anything and everything that ails ya.

"Morning, Ben." I tap the trunk button on my keys, aiming for the aluminum containers of huevos rancheros and breakfast meats.

"Back atcha, Tuck. What's got you all space cadet this morning?" His bushy mustache twitches, fighting a smile.

I roll my eyes, passing him the covered dish with Bree's turnovers. Pumpkin may not compliment my Spanish-inspired dish, but I guarantee they'll be one of the first things gone. A lot of soldiers stop by on their way to work for a free meal, but that doesn't mean they don't deserve quality.

Ben helps stack my arms full, thankfully not commenting on my heated cheeks as he closes the trunk for me. "No cadet, Sarge. Just trying to remember if I turned off the toaster this morning."

He stops. "Huh?"

I chuckle. "Pulling your leg, sir."

"Knock it off." He slaps my back... hard, jarring the trays in my hand. "I was hoping to catch you before you set up this morning."

"What's up?"

We fall into step, our natural military rhythm leading us inside the slightly dated kitchen in the rear of Sarge's converted ranch. The eighties-era home doubles as a bunkhouse for veterans, mid-transition. Those who are down on their luck, or maybe never had luck to begin with.

The next town over holds a larger, free-standing building to host bigger events and meetings, but this gateway house... this place holds my heart.

The old man's worn eyes crease with worry as I ready the buffet line on the center island for the morning crew. Silence stretches between us until I stop, bracing my hands against the counter to give my undivided attention.

A heavy sigh sinks Sarge's shoulders as he gazes down the hall toward the back bedrooms. "Got a new guy in last night. Real mess. Early twenties. Chip on his shoulder. The bartender at Barron's Distillery told him about this place before she poured him in a cab."

"Shit. What do you know about the kid?"

"Not a lot. He wasn't exactly forthcoming when he arrived. He had tags and fatigues and needed a place to sleep it off."

I nod. "What exactly do you need from me?"

A creak from the back hall stops our conversation.

When no one appears, Ben continues. "Well, Vanessa left me a message after she closed up last night. She was *hot*." His crack of laughter echoes through the kitchen, his slap to the countertop breaking the tomblike state of the kitchen. "The guy bragged on and on all night. Apparently, his burger blows theirs out of the water. And he served his entire platoon at Bragg with more flavor and speed than they serve a Podunk little town... his words."

A snort slips out, and I shake my head. "Bet that went over well."

"No doubt." Sarge goes back to helping me set up, stacking paper plates and utensils at the edge of the island to start the train. "Anyway, I thought you could, you know... have one of your chats with him. See if he actually is qualified as a chef, or if he was blowing smoke."

My brain works through the possibilities. With all the projects in the works right now, I could use help. Small towns aren't exactly flush with new employees willing to work in hot-as-hell kitchens. Especially ones with experience.

"Morning." A scratchy baritone, rough with sleep, startles us both.

"Hey!" Sarge steps forward, hand extended for a shake, while I wipe mine on a kitchen towel. "Sleep well?"

"Sure..." The kid eyes us both, as if we're the strangers in this situation. His hair sticks on end, well past the time for a haircut. Cargos hang off his narrow hips, wrinkled and dirty. An unfair amount of wear lines his youthful face. Sun damage. Scars from battle, or bar fights, not sure.

Remembering my manners, I extend a hand. "Breakfast is served, if you're hungry. I'm Tucker."

"Neil." He shakes, keeping a wary eye on me and Ben. "You fellas talking about me this morning?"

A laugh slips out. "No bullshit, I see."

"I was just telling Chef here about your late-night arrival." Ben has the decency to look chagrined.

Not me.

"Heard you got skills in the kitchen," I say, burying a large serving spoon in each tray.

With everything set for breakfast, my attention falls on the deep purple bags taking up residence under our new tenant's sable eyes, the sallow of his cheeks. The kid's had a tough few weeks, by the looks of it.

"I get by."

"A lot more modest in the light of day, huh?" Ben chuckles and the kid cocks his head, confused. "BART called." He passes the kid a plate. "Help yourself. Breakfast is casual round here. Then you boys can talk."

Neil nods distractedly. "Don't love everyone knowing my business. Especially before I've caffeinated."

God! This kid reminds me so much of Smith when he came back to town.

"*Hah!* You're in the wrong town then, buddy." Ben elbows me in the ribs, but I've never been one to shy off. I watch Neil pile two heaps of eggs on his plate and a hefty portion of sausage and bacon. How much of his appetite is hangover over hunger?

"I'm just passing through. No need for a dossier," he says, tucking into his breakfast right at the bar.

Crossing my arms, I rest a hip against the counter. "No need for distrust, either. We're here to help. Whatever you need."

"Why?"

"Why not?" I shrug a shoulder, biting back my snark when Ben narrows his wrinkled eyes. "Look, this is a safe place for veterans. Sometimes soldiers need a bed to rest, a meal, a job... We connect the dots." I wait while the kid chews his food. When he stays silent, I point at the tags hanging from his neck. "Where'd you serve, son?"

His jaw works silently. Questions glare like a neon sign in the stiffness of his body, but I wait, calling on the patience from surveillance ops during my enlisted days.

"262nd Combat Support Battalion, Sir. Hooah!"

I nod. "How long are you in town?" This guy could solve my overbooking situation.

Haunted brown eyes fall to his plate. "Couple weeks. Couple months. Not sure."

Not great, but... "How 'bout this? I'm in a pinch at my restaurant. Maybe we could help each other out."

The kid glances between me and Ben, finishing the last remnants of his breakfast as if a bear's chasing his honey. Ben beams and I shake my head, until finally Neil sets his plate on the counter, his eyes leveling me with a challenge.

"What d'ya got for me?"

Sounds of a busy kitchen break through the solitude of my back office. Pots clang. Voices shout instructions under a backdrop of jokes. Heavy metal blasts from the radio balanced on a wire shelf in the corner. The staff can party all they want until service starts. Then, their asses become well-oiled, disciplined machines.

I should be out there now, prepping my duck, checking on stations. Instead, I'm stuck in here balancing next week's schedule. Every stupid project I take on the job becomes more difficult. Every time I think I'm done; another great idea or great opportunity pops up. With a wedding, a reception, and a retirement party coming up, Smith will be out of commission. Most of the week and the entire weekend, he'll be focused on the catering side, leaving me to my first love... Two-Fourteen.

"I've got to get someone else in here," I grumble into the quiet.

Neil should have been here half an hour ago to walk through his qualifications. We chatted basics at the bunkhouse, but I wanted to see him in action before the doors opened for evening service. To figure out if I have a line chef, sous chef, or glorified salad chef.

What am I working with? And how bad is training this kid going to hurt?

"Visitor for you, Chef." My third in command taps knuckles to the frosted glass on my door, his smoke roughened voice trailing away before I can answer back.

"Come in," I say, packing away my calendar in the top drawer of my desk.

The door brushes open unapologetically. "S'up, boss."

Irritation clouds my thoughts. *I have half a mind to...* I shake my head. "Do you need a watch?"

A flash of something dark passes behind his eyes. So quick, I almost miss it. "You wanted to show me the kitchen."

As if he's doing me the favor...

Scrawny arms fold over the tattered band shirt Neil thought would be appropriate for a job interview. His hair stands on end, at least the section on top not buzzed tight to his scalp.

Not that I expected anything formal. Still... respect, man.

For a moment, I just sit there, contemplating my sanity. Do I really want to offer this kid a job? His blank face concerns me, but I don't have a lot of options. These next few months are going to kick my ass.

Sighing, I drop my head back on my shoulders, praying for patience. "Come on."

Resignation takes over as I move past the asshole and out of my dank office. Normally, the space is comfortably utilitarian, but that was before tension sucked all the air out of the room. I don't wait to see if he follows. If the kid knows what's good for him...

In the kitchen, structured chaos reigns in the clang of pots, this bawdy laughter, and instruction being called down by Smith.

"How's is looking, man?" I slap him on the back, drawing attention from the squab he's lining onto a cooling rack to rest.

"Not bad, Chef. Gotta keep an eye on the spare rib... May have to 86 that later."

I nod, watching my trusted employees prep for service with pride. Smith has the kitchen tonight. Everyone here respects that, freeing me up to plan our future. We've been a well-oiled machine for over a year now.

Instinctively, my eyes land on the pink-haired pixie in the back. My last hire to finish out our kitchen. At least before Smith started drifting down his own path. Working with her has been a year of blue balls and cold showers. Only part of which is a result of her very public swearing off men. She has no use for us.

And yet every male eye in the kitchen—except the very smitten Smith—follows her around like hyperactive puppies.

Every weekend, tight tank tops hug that lithe little body. Legging and goofy gaucho pants alternate torturing my cock, depending on her mood. Tonight's sassy black chef pants cup her finely sculpted ass the way I want my hands to. The fabric is covered in hot pink skeletons that give her a don't fuck with me vibe. One I've struggled to obey since hiring our pastry genius.

Squeezing my fist in my pocket, I take a step back, creating an opening to introduce our newbie. He smirks, eyeing our setup as if it's a cockroach crunched underneath the sole of his shoe.

"Smith, this is Neil. New to town."

"Passing through," he corrects, ignoring Smith's outstretched hand.

Knowing eyes meet mine over the kid's head, but with the small shake of mine, he lets it go.

"Neil's worked in kitchens. I thought he'd come in handy with our schedule blowing up this fall."

Smith's shoulders stiffen. "If you need more time..."

I wave him off. "Nah, man. You've worked too hard for your place." Smiling, I slap my mentee on the back, pride bolstering my shit mood. "I'm proud. Honest. The bistro's going to be a hit!" A slight tint colors Smith's tan cheeks, and I laugh. "Anyway, with your ass working fewer hours, I need some help around here."

"Yeah. Yeah." Smith's coarse chuckle draws the attention of the other chefs as he goes back to dinner prep. "Let me know if you need anything."

"What's up, boss?" Mark asks, walking over trays of baked sweet potatoes for the warmer. His dark goatee and tightly clipped hair remind me of a culinary Tony Stark, only without the swagger... or the money. He's just as genius with a grill, without the confidence of the billionaire. It's why Mark is happier as second in the kitchen and not head honcho.

Hence the need for another apron in the kitchen.

Moving to the side, I wave for Mr. Congeniality to join the conversation. "Making rounds, Iron Man. This is Neil. If everything works out, he'll join us for a bit."

Mark steps up, and this time Neil returns the handshake, glancing around at the eyes trained on us.

"Nice to meet you."

"Yeah. Ugh... What do you want me to do around here?"

"Can everyone pause a minute?"

Slowly, my staff works their way over. Even Vincent pauses with a clean basin of silverware as curious gazes flit around the group.

This is a small town. Few strangers roll through who aren't tourists. Obviously, Neil is going to spike interest. Only one fixed set of baby blues raises the hackles on the back of my neck. I grind my molars at the fascination Bree sends the new guy.

"Okay, might as well tell y'all at once. Neil, here, is testing out in the kitchen." His back stiffens, but I power on, ignoring the scowl twisting his thin lips. "He's experienced, so for the time being, Neil will rotate stations until we find his niche."

A myriad of questions rumble through the staff until I hold up a hand. "No one's job is in jeopardy. But we have a lot building outside of the restaurant and a boatload of festivals. Three this fall before the first reindeer's nose lights up. I need all hands on deck here, so Iet's make him feel welcome." Neil's wave is stilted with the rest of the team's. "Okay, everyone, get back to work."

Bree keeps a watchful gaze on our trek through the kitchen from the table that acts as her station.

Neil is quiet as we pass the large vat of lobster bisque and I take a taste. "Wanna try?" I ask, waving toward the tasting spoons. He grabs a clean one, and dips into the creaminess. It's a test. Both for his tastebuds, and to see if the smart ass can act as a constructive team player.

"Could use a little salt. Otherwise, it's solid."

I nod, adding the salt I expected before turning to eye my new employee and get down to business. "Alright, so tell me a little more about your experience."

Neil fills me in on his skills as I set up the grill station. Where he's worked. The dishes he could have made better. *Blah, blah, blah.* The styles he's fused into date-worthy dishes. On and on... Mark rolls his eyes at my side. Not that Neil notices with his diatribe of his good qualities.

"Well, that's what we do here," I say. "Romance. Hearts and flowers." Bree breezes by us with a tray of molten lava cakes. "And we leave them with a dessert they'll dream of licking off each other's body."

"Mmm... I know one body I'd happily lick chocolate off of."

Fury flashes hell fire in my veins. "No fuckin' fraternizing in the kitchen!" I growl, heading for the dry pantry.

He's on my tail, hands held up as if blocking my anger. "Day-um, man. She's yours... I get it."

"What! No!"

Heat rushes my face at his laughter, feeling my staff's eyes on my back. I turn before I say something stupid. Irritation claws inside my head as I escape into the dry pantry, the hollow thump of my rubber-soled shoes punctuating the void in the room. Neil follows me through the plastic curtain.

How obvious is my fixation on Bree if a stranger notices?

My mind races as I stare at the carefully laid out shelves. I don't really need anything here, but I snatch a bunch of garlic to cover my outburst. *I don't have time for this shit.*

When I turn, I match the kid's smirk with the no-nonsense one that rules my kitchen. "First rule, there's no hanky-panky amongst the staff." I step forward, holding his hard stare. "We are small, but mighty. I can't afford drama wrecking this ship. We're short-staffed as it is." His mouth opens and closes, but I don't wait for whatever he wants to say. I step past his wiry frame and stop at the door, swallowing down my irritation. "You want the job or not?"

Silence stretches.

He shrugs. "Why not? Beats hanging out with the old man and those sad ass soldiers at that VA house."

For the third time tonight, I contemplate punching this asshole, or myself for hiring him. *What the hell is wrong with me?*

"Alright." I toss him the heads of garlic. "Mince these. You're their bitch for the night," I say, pointing at my crew. "Help anyone and everyone who needs you. We'll talk responsibilities after service if you survive."

With that, I'm out, disappearing into my office to cool the fire in my lungs. It's taking more and more effort to pretend I don't want to caveman Bree over my shoulder and lay her on the closest horizontal surface. Kitchen rules be damned.

Chapter Three

Bree

"Runner!"

Tucker's sharp tone startles me from piping *Happy Anniversary* on the edge of my dessert plate. "*Crap!*" I gently swipe at the wayward chocolate I smeared that no longer looks like an *a*.

"Need help?"

I blow a breath to center my hand as the new guy leans over my shoulder. "I got it." Perfect cursive finishes the word, scrolling perfectly into a decorative heart before I add dots and swirls along the square edge.

"I'm good with my hands," he says, insinuation dripping from every syllable. His hand spreads on my table, as if the sight of his long fingers is enough to make me drop my panties and throw myself at him in the middle of the kitchen.

"So am I." A swoosh of caramel sauce swirling circles along the bottom of the plate proves my point. Carefully, I sit my turtle cheesecake on its perfect bed and add a sprinkle of chocolate shavings and walnut dressing.

Ignoring the overbearing presence of Neil in my space, I walk the place to the pass for the server to deliver to their table with anniversary blessings from the kitchen. It's for a couple Chef knows and I guess he's been friends with the guy for years. Not that I know many faces to put with the names in his stories.

Most of my time is spent in my cramped apartment or in this kitchen.

At my table is a large reason. I don't enjoy interacting with new people. Neil's expectant face waits for a smile, or some sort of feminine flirting. I don't do that.

"Neil! Look alive!"

Tucker's shout saves me from having to deal with the new guy's ego when I ask him to back the hell off my station. He taps his knuckles on the wood counter, his eyes lingering before sauntering toward our head chef for orders.

Tonight's atmosphere is thicker than an over-kneaded dough. Neil's presence has Chef on edge, the rest of the staff scrambling to keep orders running smooth with another body in their way. Frustration pours off Neil. I assume from working gopher duty tonight instead of our chefs kissing his gourmet ass.

Earlier, I made the mistake of smiling at the newbie, not wanting to offend our new hire. Tucker's stress level the past few months is tweaking everyone's nerves. It would be nice to have extra help in the kitchen. Unfortunately, since that smile, Neil has found excuse after excuse to drop by with unneeded assistance, and Tucker has growled with every visit. I'd be flattered if the sound didn't make me so flipping anxious. I feel like I poked a bear and didn't even mean to.

I listen to barked orders from across the room as I pull a fresh pan of table bread from the oven. It's the final push. With most of the dinner rush gone, front of the house shouldn't need more bread, which is great because dessert orders stream in fast, demanding most of my attention.

"Hey Bree…"

The sweet server Tucker hired a few months ago hovers just outside of my station, twisting a tiny, black box in her hands. "What's up, Kate?"

"Table eight has a special request." Her cheeks pink with excitement as she pops the top to show me the sparkling square gem nestled in velvet. "Isn't it pretty?"

"Sure. Very pretty." A heaviness settles in my chest.

We've gotten these *requests* during many reservations. Every time, I fix a beautiful treat around the ring with a sense of dread. *Will they say yes? Will the marriage last?* I don't know if I believe love will last forever. I've never seen it.

Instead of saying any of that out loud, I take the box and tuck it in my apron while Kate grabs the ticket for her table. "Anything special?"

She smiles, eyes gleaming as she bounces from foot to foot. "Sweet guy. Ordered our best Californian with dinner. He wants the lemon cherry Petit Fours with the ring propped in the top and a bottle of champagne when she says yes."

I lift a brow. "Confident, huh?" A soft slap hits my shoulder and I bite back a grin.

"Don't be such a cynic. He's excited." Kate crosses her arms, staring me down with a faux scowl.

I laugh. "Fine. Fine. Pretty dessert for the pretty words. Does he want the question on the plate? Or is it a two-carat surprise?"

"Surprise. He'll do all the pretty words." Kate's toothpaste smile screams victory as she watches me stack and plate the tiny squares with drizzle over the base. Carefully, I place the pricey garnish on top and in just a few minutes, have a magazine worthy creation that will hopefully bring a happy ending for the couple. At least for tonight.

Kate lifts the plate with a wink and pockets the ring box to return to our customer. "Thanks a bunch, B. I'll let you know how it goes."

I shake my head as she walks away. "Don't let her eat the ring! Can't have someone chipping a tooth on my dessert," I finish under my breath.

Tucker catches my eye from where he's plating one of the last remaining tickets. Mark says something that causes an eye roll, and he points to the back hallway, nodding his head for his second-in-command to follow that way. Scanning, I see no sign of Neil and wonder if he couldn't crack one full service.

Another ticket prints that I grab and take to my table. I don't have time to worry about the goings on in the rest of the kitchen. I have an hour left before things wind down. The faster I push out the dishes, the sooner I can clean up and get to bed.

Hours later, the crew is wiping down the countertops and stove. Vinny blasts a heavy stream of water into the dish basin, rinsing a few of the larger pots. Kate sits off to the side, rolling silverware with another server. The place smells of cleaning solution and mop water instead of the delicious scents of roasted meat and fresh baked yummies in my section.

Everyone minds their own business, knocking out closing duties diligently. Mark has a pair of earbuds in his ears, ignoring us all. After scrubbing my table, I pack away the few leftovers we have in one of the silver trays Tucker takes with him to the VA, covering the sweets with foil for easy refrigeration.

"How'd it go?" Neil's smokey voice rumbles way too close to my ear and I jump.

"What the hell?" A smarmy smile crinkles the corners of his eyes, earning a glare from me. "I don't like being startled," I say, hoping he gets the hint.

"Aww, don't be like that. I just wanted to see how your night went. Looked like you made a happy couple's evening."

To his credit, Neil backs far enough away to prop a hip against my table and watch me straighten up. He does nothing to help, only crosses his scrawny arms and waits. Every trip to the trash, I have to step around him, making even the easy tasks take forever. *Freaking annoying.*

"Do you need something?" I ask, trying my best to sound friendly.

He shrugs. "Nah, thought I'd walk you to your car. It's late, you know."

Surprised, I glance up at the rest of the kitchen. Everyone's gone. "Holy crap! I must have gotten distracted."

Neil chuckles, the sound forced and awkward in the silence of the empty space. "So, how bout it? Walk you out?" I swallow, wracking my brain for a tasteful way to say no. "Come on. Can't be too careful with the strangers out there." His smirk adds to the uncomfortable feeling tightening my chest at being in here alone.

"Um... you're a stranger, too. And this town has all of a thousand people. Sixty percent who are over fifty."

"I promise, I'm a boy scout."

Something about Neil's demeanor gives me the creeps. Which is stupid. Past issues popping up to judge someone who's done nothing wrong.

"Fine," I say, reaching under the counter for my purse and keys. The quicker I get out of here, the sooner I can shake this odd paranoia. "Let's go."

Chapter Four

Tucker

Voices grow louder in the hallway outside my office, drawing my attention away from the never-ending cash receipts I'm trying to enter into the accounting software. I hate this part of the job. Rubbing the exhaustion from my eyes doesn't help focus any better, either.

Neil's deep timber drawls something too low for me to hear. The yellow sticky note on my desk scribbled with *background check* sticks out like a sore thumb. Tonight, he was irritating, but the kid seems to know his way around the kitchen. Maybe I shouldn't be such a hardass. I'm debating crumpling the reminder when a husky laugh cuts through the silence, loud and clear.

"What the fuck?"

I'm out of my chair before I second guess the decision. Ripping the door open stops Neil and Bree in their tracks.

"Tuck… Chef… you scared the hell out of me." Bree's hand falls to her chest and I try to not take notice of the slight curve panting under those delicate fingers.

"Heard noises. Thought everyone was gone for the night." Shit. I sound like a caveman. Can't string a full sentence together with Neil standing unprofessionally close to the woman who makes my blood boil with cravings I shouldn't have. I warned him.

Neil's face is stone. "We're the last ones out, boss."

Bree glances between the two of us glaring, confusion dipping her brows. She slides a few inches away, giving the testosterone room to breathe.

"I thought everyone was gone," I say, catching these jade-colored eyes. Their beauty is suffocating. But I can't have her. I should let her go. I glance at Neil. Not to him, though.

He clears his throat. "Now, they are. I was just walking Bree to her car." He slides his hand to her lower back, staking claim.

I bite off a growl as Bree scoffs, sliding out of his reach. *Good, girl.*

I grab her elbow, tugging her to my side. "You go ahead. I need to discuss a menu with Bree for next week."

He pauses. "What's up? I've got ideas for menus that would knock the socks off that prime rib."

My jaw grinds on my back teeth. *Lord, give me strength not to go to jail tonight.*

"We've got it. It's dessert related for upcoming parties." Those beady little eyes narrow and I want to cheer. "Bye, now." Without waiting for his response, I tug Bree inside my office and close the door.

She rips her arm away. "Was that necessary?"

"Was what necessary? We need to discuss the bourbon reception next week." Stalking to the other side of my desk, I ignore the daggers lancing my back and the fuming vixen staring me down with crossed arms and prickly armor. "Have you looked over the calendar I emailed last week?"

Her arms fall. "You emailed a calendar?"

It's a total excuse, but works for why I need Bree in my office. "I'm trying something new for the fall, to keep everyone on the same page with all the jobs in the air."

"Do you need me for something?"

Spit lodges in my throat, choking on answers younger me would have had for that question. I cough to clear the airway, my eyes watering as they lock on the smirking hellcat in front of me.

"We've got receptions and parties coming up in the next few weeks, and Smith will be busy with his grand opening. I need everyone on point with orders and inventory to make sure we don't fall behind."

She nods, the pink bob I want to run my fingers through bouncing around her chin. That spunky hair just highlights another damn reason I should keep my filthy thoughts to myself. She's bright light and spunk. Quirky. After a hard life, Bree deserves the best of everything.

What the hell would a young, beautiful woman at the beginning of her career want with a tired old chef with more responsibilities than time?

"I'll get on that. Any special requests?"

Yes!

"No. I'm still planning menus and I've appointment after appointment with brides and organizers for all this crap."

"Okay then…" She cocks her head at me like I've lost my mind. "What is it?"

"Did this really need…" Her agitated hand waves circles toward the door. "All of that?"

Bracing my fists on the desk, I lean over, meeting Bree's challenging gaze. "All of what, Bree? You don't normally need help walking to your car. Did you want to go with Neil? Was that some sparkling conversation I interrupted?"

"*Psh!* Don't be an ass. You know very well what you were doing."

Annoyance colors every word, piquing my interest. "What was I doing, Bree?" That upturned chin begs for my fingers. The fire sharpening those cat-like eyes promises an explosion of passion. One I'm desperate to give.

"Y-you guys were pounding chest and grunting like idiots. You practically peed a circle around my legs."

"Hah!" Screw the safety of my desk. Moving slowly, I stalk to the other side, holding Bree's stare. "Don't think I'm into that sort of thing, Bree. Though, you say the word… I'm willing to try almost anything." I stop right in front of her, toe to non-slip toe. "How bout if we avoid bodily fluids though, huh?"

"Ack! Don't be gross." She smacks my stomach… hard, and I grab her hand, holding it against the front of my restaurant polo. I ditched the jacket the moment service was done. Now, there's a single layer of fabric separating her hot palm from the ridges of my stomach, and I have never been happier about having a best friend who owns a gym at my age.

"What are we doing here, Tucker?" Her breath catches, barely louder than a whisper over the blood pumping through my ears.

"Something dangerous, Bree. Something a long time coming." I lean closer, giving her all the time to run, the opportunity to slap me silly, which is what she should do. My vision narrows in on the peachy color of her lips, wondering if they taste as sweet as they look. I hook that plump lower under my thumb and tug gently. "Tell me to stop."

Bree's velvety pink tongue flicks out, wetting that lip. I moan, lifting the bottom of her chin to read those expressive eyes. Searching gives not an ounce of doubt, only excitement and frustrations, and... heat.

Her fist tightens against my stomach when I pause, inches from heaven. "You stop now; I'll bury you in my Hobart."

Chuckling, I dip, capturing that sassy mouth the way I've wanted to for a year. The softness gives easily, parting immediately under the pressure of pent-up need. My only thought is, *what the hell took me so long?*

Well, that's not my only thought.

Bree lifts on her toes, making devouring her sweetness easier and I take full advantage, keeping my hands locked on her face to prevent roaming. Our kiss explodes on impact, setting off every craving I've denied since meeting this spunky beauty. She swipes her tongue across mine and my cock feels the motion, tapping against the back of my zipper to get in on this action. *No fucking way.*

I lock my hands behind that veil on pink cotton candy at the back of her neck and devour every ounce she gives. Every heated caress tests my restraint, undermining my ability to keep a rein on the kiss and not let a year's-worth of backed up hormones take over.

Sampling the chocolate and lemon tart lingering on her lips is a startling reminder that only a few hours ago, Bree was cooking her ass off for my restaurant.

My employee.

Shit!

Pulling back, I rest my forehead against hers. "We shouldn't do this."

"Too late. Why haven't we done this before?" Her breath tickles my chin, just before she bites it.

"What the hell, woman?"

"Just keeping you in the right head space." Her delighted chuckle releases a bit of the tightness in my shoulders. "I know this is... complicated."

"Yeah, complicated." Leaning back, I plead with her to understand. "I'm your boss. There are implications, Bree. Plus, you're—" I wave a hand up and down her body and she narrows her eyes.

"I'm what, Tucker?" Bree's brows disappear into her hairline. Her hip cocking to the side with enough sass to lay me on my ass.

"You're young."

She crosses her arms. "Do you want me to say you're old?"

I snort. "No! But—"

"Look, I'm twenty-five, not fifteen. I'm not some little girl who doesn't know what she wants. I make my own decisions. Have been for the majority of those years." A cloud passes behind her eyes that brings me closer, crowding her space to offer comfort. She sighs, dropping her arms from their defensive position to rest on my chest. Her voice is guarded, quietly protecting herself without meeting my eyes. "I've lived more life than most people twice my age. This doesn't have to be anything big. You know, I think you're hot. Obviously. You're mid-forties, Tucker. Not some skeevy old man."

My hands gravitate to the soft curve of hip driving me crazy and pull her into my space as I rest my rear end on the edge of my desk. "You drive me absolutely crazy, Bree. Watching you. Wanting you. I tried to talk myself out of hiring you, just so I didn't have to deal with the torture of you flouncing through my kitchen in those little bitty tank tops under your chef's jacket."

"What!" she screeches. "You weren't going to hire me?"

A laugh slips out despite her pissed scowl. "Self-preservation. I swear. But I'm more than happy that I did. At least until a more age-appropriate asshole puts the moves on you, and I want to slice off all his cooking fingers with my butcher knife."

"*Hah!* Wow. Okay." She shakes her head, stepping between my knees to get closer. "You know, it may say something completely crazy about me that I dig this whole caveman schtick. Within reason."

I hold my hands up by my head innocently as her finger digs into my chest, but I love this spunk. Especially over that sad expression she had. One I want to know more about.

Looking away, I wrack my brain for how this won't end it in an epic disaster. "Look, Bree, the next few weeks are chaos. There's a reason I don't date. I don't have time." My heart rate spikes with how much I need to get done this week. "It'd be unfair to you."

She stops me with a hand on my cheek. "I don't need a proper date or promises of forever. I only thought we could stop with this, will they or won't they dance, and have a little fun." Stressed ticks at the corner of her jaw and I hate it. She swallows. "As long as it doesn't affect my job."

The question hits with such vulnerability that it pisses me off. "What the hell, Bree... I'd never—"

She stops me with a finger to my lip before smiling and edging away. Every inch of distance feels wrong. I barely got my hands on her. "Where does that leave us?" I ask, hating the flash of high school memories that hit me like a ton of bricks.

That beautiful smile eases some of the tension in my neck. There's a reason I was a player when I left the military. Having a different woman every weekend kept all these nasty feelings out of the way. Now, I've pined for one who was unattainable for so long that when she's offering herself up to me like a decadent crème brûlée to sample, all I can think of is it's not enough.

"Why don't we survive this weekend and touch base on Monday, since the restaurant is closed? Maybe we can connect for dinner at a place where neither of us needs an oven mitt."

"Sounds good." I exhale and bend to take another sample of that teasing smile. My lips linger against hers, breathing in that decadent bakery scent. "See you tomorrow, Bree."

"Ugh!" Bree looks to the ceiling, seemingly as frustrated as I feel to not get my hands on her tonight. "See you tomorrow, Chef." I nod at the return to formal rolls, dropping my eyes to the sexy sway of ass walking out my door. Before she's out of earshot, I catch her groan. "God! I'm going to need new batteries tonight," she says under her breath and I burst out with laughter.

Going around to my desk chair, I adjust a boner the size of Texas, and revel in the renewed energy to take on the day and my massive to-do list tomorrow.

Chapter Five

Bree

Pulling at the massive oak door, I let myself into the newest distillery in town. The one throwing their grand opening celebration on the rooftop of *Two-Fourteen* in two weeks. At least, per Tucker's emailed calendar.

Which is why I'm standing in the middle of a brand new tasting room with rich wood and disinfectant assaulting my senses. The silence is eerie, unlike the chaos in our kitchen. I have no idea why I thought this would be a good idea, considering how little I like people. I'm hoping if I can take some of the stress off the boss, it'll have some trickle-down effect toward knocking the rust off my love-life.

Well... bedroom-life, at least.

"Hello..."

I skip right over the overstuffed leather chairs and wingbacks, and slide onto a wooden stool at the bar. The angle overlooks a massive back room full of stainless-steel barrels and pipes. Almost like a spy with the massive, floor-to-ceiling windows giving patrons a perfect view of their entire operation.

There's not a nick in sight. No wear on the shiny chrome. The place looks so stinking clean, I'm afraid to touch anything. Even first thing in the morning, flour and dough balls contaminate my hands.

Bright afternoon sunlight streams through the warehouse windows, freshening what could be a stuffy tasting room, if not for the chrome accents and fresh white hydrangeas decorating every barrel table.

"Welcome!" The backroom door swings open, startling me as a smiling cowboy Barbie greets me with an armload of heavy glass bottles. Gently, she sets them on the empty counter. "What can I do you for?" she asks, wiping what I assume is non-existent dust from her hands.

I cock my head at the odd greeting, but the woman's infectious smile is impossible not to return, even if it's more of a professional greeting. Being here on business—and as a favor to the boss—makes frowning like I rolled naked through a field of heel spurs not the best first impression.

"Is the owner working today?" I ask, trying not to let the woman's perfection and pretty, heart-shaped face irk my nerves. Her straw hat screams hillbilly uniform—something I'd never be caught dead in—except, with the high-end weave and matching boots, she looks anything but.

Barbie smirks, organizing the fresh stash of brown liquor behind the bar. "My cousin is always here."

I snort. "I know the type."

"Right..."

"Lex! Visitor!"

A clatter in the back sets off a chain of curses and clangs. I cringe, having created a bit of chaos and clumsiness in the kitchen many times. The door swings wide in front of a hurricane of blonde hair and an almost identical face to the one behind the bar.

"Wow! You two could be twins."

An unladylike sound escapes the hurricane, and Barbie slaps her shoulder. "Our moms are twins, so... you know..." She flicks her thumb back and forth between them with a grin before leaning elbows on the butcher block in front of me. "So, how can I help you?"

"Well," I place my hands in my lap, hiding my picked apart cuticles. "My boss sent me... or well, I volunteered this morning when he had a minor conniption over a shipment and nearly yanked out half his hair." Their mouths drop and I ramble on, wishing I were back in my safe, anti-social corner of the kitchen.

"Apparently, someone glitched on this week's produce order, and now Chef has no eggplants for his eggplant parmesan. Five bushels of eggs won't go far in the Italian wedding reception booked for Friday night. I mean, I'll use them in my desserts eventually, but Chef wasn't happy, and now he's scrambling because it's the bride's favorite dish and apparently, their *small* family reception includes fifty people."

Done with my rant, I suck in my missing oxygen, and thank Barbie for the glass of water she sets in front of me.

"Big family," she says, propping up beside her cousin.

Both women stare at me like I'm a puzzle, setting me on edge as I tuck my hair, overgrown pink tips and all, behind my ears. I wish I weren't so awkward around pretty people. Maybe I shouldn't have told them about failed orders. It makes us sound like amateurs.

"Yeah, so anyway, I'm here to feel out details for your party, not to vent over someone else's." The empty room draws my attention. "Have y'all had your grand opening yet?"

Lexi straightens, taking in the warm, wood oasis she's created. A line forms between her brows, highlighting just how much stress the woman is under building a new business. "Soon. That's what this party is for... thanking my team for their hard work."

"That's very nice of you."

She shrugs, her face a lovely shade of tomato. "Yeah, well. This place was my husband's dream. I couldn't have pulled it off without my family. They busted their asses getting this place ready." Lexi's voice clogs, and she turns away.

I open my mouth, but Barbie shakes her head.

"We thought everyone deserved a celebration before things kick into high gear." She smirks and pushes Lexi's shoulder, distracting her out of sad thoughts. "Somewhere not here."

Lexi chuckles stiffly. "My staff shouldn't work their own party."

"Yes. Plus, we want food that's not roasted peanuts and pretzels." Barbie smirks as she walks to the end of the bar and brings back three half-empty bottles of amber colored liquids. "These are our theme for the party."

A rich navy label circles each bottle with the distillery's logo embossed in silver. A single-word name scrolls across the front. Lexi's face softens as she studies the first one. "My husband made notes before he passed, and his brother helped me create the perfect bourbon recipe from those. Little tweaks here and there, you know." She swallows thickly. "Do you like bourbon?"

"Could I live in Kentucky if I didn't?" Okay, that's a minor lie, but we share a laugh, easing the lingering stiffness between strangers.

"Here." Lexi pours an ounce of each liquid into tasting glasses and slides them across the bar. "Tucker talked about pairing his food with our specialty castes. Doing more of a tasting dinner. Are you his head chef?"

My ears heat. "No. I'm the dessert queen. Just here because whining supplier equals nuclear kitchen, equals pre-mature bald spot on Chef."

Barbie giggles. "That'd be a damn shame. He is one sexy daddy."

Confused, I squint at the naughty glint in the young girl's eyes. "He doesn't have k—oh!" My face flames, a flash of jealousy rotting the acid in my stomach.

Lexi swats her cousin, rolling her eyes as she points left to right. "Anyway... we thought we'd pair in this order. Appetizer. Entrée. Dessert."

I smile at her obvious pride and sniff the first glass. "Citrus?" She beams, and immediately ingredients run through my head that would pair beautifully. "Shit!" I yank my phone out of my back pocket and open the note app, rambling off recipes while the ladies watch in awe. "Orange-glazed lollipops would be a-maz-ing with this."

"Lollipops?" The scrunch in Barbie's brow makes her look even younger, and I chuckle.

"Fancy way to say chicken legs."

"Ooo... Gordon Ramsay style?"

I snort, my face flushing hot with embarrassment. "Not the best thing to say in front of chef, but if you do, please let me be there." I make a face that cracks them up harder, and pride fills my chest as I move to taste the next bourbon.

Notes of detected flavors flow easily from my fingers while Lexi entertains me with stories of her husband. His fixation on brewing perfection seems prolific. All the nights he kept her up visualizing his dream. The hopes for their distillery and the sacrifices they made to get there. Love and sadness cloud her eyes until a door slamming and a muffled curse draws her attention to the floor-to-ceiling windows. A dark-haired man stomps through the brewing room, agitated by something on the dials.

"I'm going to leave you ladies to taste while I check on things." Lexi nods at the glasses. Her smile is strained as she backs away, eyeing her cousin in silent communication. "I gave Tucker carte blanche. I trust y'all will make something bad ass, so my crew doesn't ditch me opening weekend." She shrugs. "They may want to punch me in the face, but maybe if we butter them up, they won't throw me in one of the aging barrels."

We chuckle, watching her path toward the disgruntled employee, before the woman who I will forever think of as Cowboy Barbie goes into her sales spiel, listing off qualities and sourcing for my next glass.

One whiff and I'm imagining the savory, charred brisket that would complement the drink perfectly, though the first sip burns the back of my throat, triggering a cough that's impossible to hide. A glass of water appears in front of me. "Thanks," I croak, sliding the dry bourbon back across the bar. "That one's a little out of my element."

Barbie snickers, tapping her hot pink nail to the last glass. "Me too. Try this."

Her excitement distracts from the fact that I'm two shots to the wind without a lick of food in my stomach. Taste testing before work may not have been the best idea I've ever had. I just wanted to take one thing off Tucker's overly stressed broad shoulders.

As if sensing my need, she scoops a bowl of salted cashews and sets them beside me. "Thanks." I grin at my new friend. "You're like clairvoyant Bartender Barbie."

"Hah! Too funny. And I'm just now realizing I never introduced myself." She holds a hand out. "I'm Elle. I work in a distillery, and I hate bourbon."

Chuckling, I shake her hand. "I'm Bree. I make insane desserts. And I pray this is the last sip of Kentucky bourbon I'll have for a while." The tension I walked in with has evaporated. Still, I eye the glass she slides closer like a snake ready to bite. "My drinks don't usually pack this much punch, Elle."

"Try it."

She laughs at the face I make, but to my surprise, the last sample is missing that blow-out-your-eyeballs quality. A pleasant blast of cocoa and espresso coats my tongue instead, and I hum. "Holy shit! It's chocolate heaven without that... kerosene taste."

Elle's face lights up. "You don't really like bourbon, do you?"

A cough slips past that I hide in my napkin. "What clued you in?"

For the next hour, while I down a glass of water and black coffee, Elle tells me a bit about Lexi's history getting the distillery open, their struggle to learn the process, and the people who pitched in. By the end, I'm motivated to create a menu these people deserve.

Two-Fourteen is going to blow this party out of the water.

Chapter Six

Tucker

Smoke billows from the sides of the oven, filling my kitchen with a noxious odor.

"Shit!" Dropping my cast iron on the cooktop, I rush to turn the heat off. "Mark! Watch the grill." Curses fly as I snatch my mitts and grab the tray of steaming and exploded potatoes. They hit the trashcan with a hiss, and I growl. "Where the fuck is Neil?"

"No clue, boss." My sous chef is wise to stay out of my war path. He busies himself with monitoring my pans, his face relaxing when I head for the pantry and he's out of my line of fire.

The rest of my crew bustles about the kitchen, chopping, organizing, and setting up service. It's chaos. Unfortunately, not the one person who should be showing up and showing out is nowhere to be found. I'd hoped to keep a close eye on the kid tonight. Evaluate if the pain in my ass is worth the hemorrhoid.

I breathe a sigh of relief that the rest of my kitchen runs efficiently. Except another missing link which is bugging me more than

I'd like. A flouncy pink bob is noticeably absent from my world tonight, and I don't like it.

Without being asked, Vinny hurries my burned sheet pan to the sink and starts scrubbing. "Thanks, man." I swallow.

"You got it, boss."

With my arms loaded with potatoes, I head to the prep sink and dump them in before I go in search of my missing chef. Before I can though, Bree rushes by, casting a worried glance at our smoke-filled oven on the way to her station. Neil is seconds behind her. *What the hell?*

"Where the fuck have you been?" I growl, grinding my teeth.

Neil strolls by without a care, right up to the wide open oven. "Who touched my potatoes?"

"You gotta be fuckin' kidding me?" Mark growls, storming to the back with my cast iron. I trust my man to prep my entrée for what I need.

Crossing my arms, I stare down Neil. "I asked you a question."

His gaze passes over Bree before landing on me. "I was having a cig. What's the big deal?"

"The big deal is I thought you were a chef, and you can't cook a fuckin' baked potato."

"Come the fuck on... I took a break. Sue me. One of you assholes couldn't look in on my food?"

My crew roll their eyes, but the cocksure new chef lights my insides on fire. "It's not their job, but someone *would* have if you'd thought to ask." All eyes are on our standoff, all sound coming to a standstill in the busy kitchen. "Tell me now... Are you worth wasting my time on?"

"Fuck you!" His fists ball at his side and he looks about ready to take a swing when hot pink fingernails curl around his elbow and ease him back.

"Why don't you boys save the big talks until after service?"

If I could rip Bree's freaking hand off Neil without hurting her, I would. An overwhelming desperation to separate the two is the only reason I find myself nodding over the roaring in my ears.

"Back to work, everyone!"

Neil offers Bree a grateful smile, adding fuel to the fire that will burn him later.

Thankfully, the rest of the night runs as smooth as possible with my staff tiptoeing around a land mine. When the restaurant closes, Neil is the first one out after his shift work, not even stopping to make right on our earlier argument or beg for his job.

I make my way to the section entirely taken over by Bree before she can escape as well. She's always the last one out. Every single weekend. But I have no idea the state of her mind, or if she made plans with Neil after work. Both of them walking in at the same moment has tortured me with what-ifs all night.

"See me after everyone's gone. I'll give you a ride home."

She opens her mouth, but self-preservation forces my feet to move before I do something stupid with so many eyeballs around us.

At my desk, I listen to every slam of the security door at the back of the restaurant, counting. Guilt stabs my conscience, knowing I should be out there instead of hiding in here under the guise of paperwork. I do anyway though. Screw responsibilities. Ever since that kiss, my mind has had a one track focus.

In my head, I see the order of every person walking to their car. The servers are generally done first, with the line chef and Mark close behind. Vinny takes a bit longer to mop the floors, but eventually my silent headcount leaves one person I'm itching to see.

A light sheen of sweat breaks out on my hands as I wait. My office has never looked so drab. Beige walls. Cheap Berber carpet. Dark wood paneling on the lower half of the walls. Effective chair rail. Shitty décor.

After what feels like forever, a knock sounds at my door and I get up, grabbing my keys and jacket from the chair before I answer it. Ants crawl up my spine, pushing me to move, unwilling to wait to be in her presence for another second. Bree's shocked expression schools the moment I step through the door and cup her elbow, turning for the exit.

"What the... Chef?"

I keep walking, my steps hurried. "Yes?"

"I thought... I thought we had a meeting." She tries to dig in her heels as we reach the back door, and I let her pause.

"Do you have everything you need?"

Her lips open and close a few times with no sound. "Y-yes."

"Then let's go. We can talk over mac-n-cheese at my place."

"Wha—"

I don't let her finish the sentence. Stepping forward, I slam Bree's mouth with my own, taking away all brain function with the first swipe of my tongue. I shouldn't be too rough, but I didn't want to hear excuses. Now that I made the decision, all I could think about was having her.

Bree's lips part on a sigh, soothing some of the anxiety tightening my muscles. I dip inside, exploring the sweet recesses of this woman's mouth. Almost immediately, the frantic kiss softens into something sensual, a dance of tongues and lingering strokes of lips. My cock stiffens, stealing all train of thought. Her delicate fingers scratch through the back of my hair and I groan, pulling back to not maul her against the wall of my restaurant.

Our breath mingles as I rest my forehead against Bree's, praying this isn't a stupid decision. "If you want me to take you home..."

"No." The word is barely a whisper, but it's all I need.

Twining our fingers, my self-control cracks and I hurry her out the door and into my old Jeep Cherokee before she changes her mind. In the dark, I contemplate how to phrase the question that has eaten me up all night. Bree's thumbs tap out an impatient beat on her thigh, the glow from the streetlamp highlighting that soft curve of her cheekbone. I can't resist. I reach the back of my fingers to smooth down that beautiful line.

"I have to ask you something."

"Nothing's stopping you," she says, all sass and sarcasm, despite the vulnerability shining in those gorgeous green eyes.

"Were you with Neil earlier?"

"Wha—! What the hell are you talking about?"

"Before service. You were late, and then both of you came in together." I rush the words, feeling awkward as hell. They also taste like ash in my mouth and I'd rather not think about the two of them together longer than necessary.

To my surprise, instead of an answer, Bree's laughter echoes in my truck, her head falling to the headrest as a hand cups her stomach to hold the shaking. She doesn't try to stop the loud guffaws, merely bends at the waist, with tears slipping from the corner of her eyes.

"Why on Earth would you think that?" she asks finally when she catches a breath.

I stutter. "You came in together. You were late." It makes sense in my head, even if I hate it.

Those sharp eyes turn on me, all sense of humor draining from the car. Bree's elbows lean across my console, her hand coming to rest on my chest with a few light slaps. "Has all the blood in your head drained south?"

I glance down, making sure she can't see the state of my half-stiff cock in the dark.

She chuckles. "I just mean that you'd think I'd give Neil the time of day. Especially in the same week I kissed you."

"You pulled him away so I wouldn't kick his ass."

"I pulled him away so you wouldn't get in *trouble* for kicking his ass."

"Okay, starting to feel like an idiot here."

With that, her lyrical giggle fills my truck, and she wraps her fist in front of my shirt, dragging me closer. "I know how you could make it up to me."

"Mmm… that I can handle." Leaning forward, I cup the side of her face, dragging her chocolate scented neck in to devour. That tender skin calls for my mark and I inhale. "How the hell do you smell like brownies every damn day?" Another taste releases a throaty moan that vibrates under my lips as I move up the column of her neck. I nibble across her jawline to those kiss-swollen lips and dive in for more, feeding the frenzy growing below my belt.

"What d'ya say we take this somewhere more comfortable?"

Her pupils have blown wide, her voice husky when she finally answers. "Sounds like a plan, big man. Get us out of here."

Chapter Seven

Bree

The ride to Tucker's house is short, filled with nerves raking across my skin that make it near impossible to sit still in his passenger seat. Country music hums low in the background, barely audible over the sound of my own breathing. Outside, the silence casts the world in an eerie glow. Even the stars in the sky hide behind wisps of clouds.

I glance over, watching Tucker's profile brighten in the light of the full moon as he drives at a safe thirty-five miles per hour out of our sleepy downtown. His death grip on my hand over the center console is grounding, given that it feels like we're the only two people alive at this hour.

"I'm just realizing now that I have no idea where you live."

He chuckles. "On purpose. The idea of you in my space is too dangerous."

My heart sinks. "So you're taking me home?"

"*Hah!* Not a chance." Tucker's heated gaze strips me raw. "Unless you changed your mind. If not, we're hiding in my house and not coming up for air until the world comes knocking."

"What about your to-do list?" I ask, refusing to admit how excited his promise makes me.

His eyes shutter briefly before he shakes his head and turns that gorgeous grin my way. "It'll be there tomorrow, right?"

I nod, my heart rate kicking up as Tucker turns onto a gravel driveway that curves behind a two-story Victorian. Sage paint gives the home an updated quality that pops the soft cream shutters and wrap-around porch. Simple ferns strategically hang from the ceiling, giving his home life. It's traditional and quaint, but more stylish than I'd expect from a busy bachelor.

"Wow! Your home is beautiful." And also points out our drastically different points of life.

"Thank you," Tucker says shyly.

He's out of the car and opening my door before I'm done taking in his pristine backyard. A white, knee-high fence separates vertical plants and raised boxes on the side of his detached single-car garage. I'd love to take a closer look, but Tucker's outstretched hand promises to deliver on the fire burning in those hazel eyes.

Once outside the car, Tucker shuts the door and presses my back into it. His thick fingers press under my chin, holding my gaze. "If you change your mind, tell me and I'll drive you home. No issue. Whatever happens—or doesn't happen—in there has no effect on your job. I need you to know that."

Protectiveness poured off him, and incredible restraint, even with the sizable erection pressing into my lower belly. It's all I can do to nod, my voice suddenly absent in the face of leaping off this bridge. Sex in the past has been just that, sex. Sometimes good, sometimes not. Tucker seems like a light shining on my world that I'm not sure I'm ready for.

However, the idea of never knowing, never experiencing the kind of combustible connection Tucker offers with every touch of his lips... "Yes. I get it."

Tucker seals our mouths, lifting the back of my thighs until they wrap his much larger frame. We move as one across his yard, up the steps, and right into his house.

"You don't lock your door!" I shriek, pulling my face away from the swollen lips kissing me senseless.

He lifts a shoulder. "Small town."

My mouth falls open with a squeak that Tucker catches as he kicks the door closed with the backside of his boot. "That doesn't mean you let anybody under the sun walk in your house."

"Are you worried about my safety, sugar?"

He grins against my throat, lips moving everywhere. My jaw. That spot behind my ear. My collarbone. I groan, wiggling my hips instinctively. Tucker's moans, and a flush of new wetness coating my panties. I'm thankful my thick chef's pants hide how desperately I want my boss, but my light tank top has no chance of covering my stiff nipples.

On nights when I know my jacket will stay on in the kitchen, I skip the bra. My breasts aren't big enough for it to matter.

Tucker's jacket is gone, too, leaving one of his signature Henley's open at the neck. The deep navy sets off his tanned skin covered in a mat of chest hair that he keeps neatly trimmed. My fingers itch to stroke the area, so I do, reveling in the freedom to explore I've never had before.

Carefully, I unbutton the remaining buttons, revealing more taut skin for my eyes. Tucker chuckles, his confident stride carrying me through the house to a set of stairs in the back. With my focus blurred under a haze of lust, I don't see an inch of his space, but I couldn't care less at this point. Until those strong fingertips grip the meat of my rear end and haul my weight higher to the packed muscles on his abdomen.

"Put me down. You're going to fall."

He swats my ass. "Not even. Shush, woman."

To prove his point, Tucker tosses my hips, catching them in one hand easily while I scream and latch onto his shoulders. His laughter reverberates off the walls, and I narrow my eyes, squeezing my thighs to lift off his chest. Knowing he has my weight, I lean back and rip my tank top over my head, watching with delight as his pupils dilate and the smile falls from his face.

His callused hand strokes up my back sensuously, holding me for his gaze. My heart drops to the bottom of my stomach as I wait for his response. I'm not altogether self-conscious, but I'm well aware that I don't have the hourglass figure men love.

Thankfully, Tucker eases my worries fast.

"You're beautiful..." His breath tickles down my breastbone, his nose brushing across the slight swell of my chest. Teasing. Never quite going where I need him.

I grab the side of his head, tugging and arching for him to hit that needy spot.

"Is my sugar impatient?" he asks, his voice rumbling against my sternum as he licks the skin north.

"Tucker!" My voice sounds whiny to my ears, needy. And finally he takes pity on me and latches onto my aching nipple, humming against the flesh as he flicks it with his tongue. Lighting sparks behind my eyelids and I close them to the heavenly assault.

Suddenly, his mouth is gone and my weight flies through the air. My eyes spring open as I bounce on a soft mattress, the sight in front of me taking my breath away. A lamp casts a dull glow in the masculine bedroom, giving off just enough light to take in the wildness in Tucker's eyes. His hair sticks out from his head, disheveled from my hands. His face is flushed. Chest heaving as he pants.

His hands grip the elastic at my waist and pauses. "You still good?"

"One hundred... Now, come on."

Impatiently, I help him get rid of my pants, the exoticness of being fully naked while he's fully clothed getting the best of me. I reach for his shirt, barely getting my hands underneath when he shoves my shoulder, toppling me backwards with a shake of his head.

"Uh uh... no way." Tucker climbs on top of me, lifting my hands until one of his traps my wrists.

I groan. "Come on... I need to touch you."

"You touch me and this will be over too fast."

Pleasure swells in my chest, but I wiggle for freedom, setting off a string of sensations that I feel every spot where our bodies align. Where the rough fabric of his shirt grazes my sensitive nipples. I gasp, and Tucker shifts his weight to the side, so he's not squishing me. His free hand strokes down my side, stopping at my hip.

"Tucker... I want..." Curling my leg, I tilt up, saying without the words.

He grins. "Good." Bending, he captures a nipple, suctioning each needy breast, back and forth. "I need you wanting, crazy and achy. Because Bree... you're going to have to forgive me when I get inside you. I've wanted you too long." He grips my hip, grinding my center against his thigh.

"Tuck... please."

He captures my plea in a heated kiss and I give him all the pent-up frustration he's giving me. I bite that lower lip, tugging and then soothing it when Tucker moans. His hips pulse, pressing into my middle, and he finally releases my hands, letting him roam across my curves, digging divots that drive me insane.

I reach for the bottom of his shirt, and he helps me tug it over his head before settling between my legs, out of reach. A frustrated groan slips out.

"Tucker! Come here... you don't have to—ahh!"

At the first swipe of Tucker's tongue, I lose all thought. He covers me with his whole mouth, swallowing my wetness with a moan that shakes my core. No part of me goes untouched. That talented tongue swirls my clit, driving me higher and higher. Animalistic noises echo through the room that will be embarrassing later, I'm sure.

But holy fuckin' oral, Batman! Tucker's mouth wins a gold freaking medal.

In no time, my body explodes. "Tuck!"

"Yes, baby!" He licks me through my high. "Say my name, again."

"Tucker! Enough." Gripping his hair, I pull those talented lips up to mine, heat rushing to my ears when I taste myself. "Please tell me you have protection... I'm not on the pill."

"Two seconds..."

Tucker disappears into the attached bathroom and the sound of slamming drawers draws my attention. *Please have a box.* I don't want to think about Tucker and other women, but I've never wanted a man to be prepared more.

After a few minutes, he walks out, wrapper in hand, and I exhale audibly. "Thank God."

A brilliant smile lights up his face. "Amen."

Chapter Eight

♥

Tucker

Watching Bree crawl to the edge of my bed, naked as the day she was born, will forever live in my spank bank.

I've heard her joke before about her petite frame or the fact that she made a career out of treats to try to grow herself some curves. I don't know what the fuck she's talking about. She's goddamn gorgeous.

It takes every ounce of my self-control to not blow my load like a teenager when her tiny hand slips inside my favorite baggy pants to stroke my swollen length. A hiss slips out and I jerk the annoying pants the rest of the way down and kick them off with my shoes. Bree giggles at my frenzy and it eases some of the chaos swirling in my blood.

She snatches the condom I'm lucky I found and unrolls the constricting rubber down my cock. Her hand tracks up and down once, twice, until I can't take anymore. Lifting under her arms, I toss Bree toward my pillows before I embarrass myself.

Dropping kisses along her abdomen, I settle myself between the most supple thighs I've gotten my hands on and spread them wider. Bree wraps her arms around my neck and brings me closer. Her scent feeds my need like a damn addict, and I want to wallow in it.

The confidence in those emerald eyes shines bright, leaving no room for doubt or questions as I slide home, burying myself in Bree's warmth. "So good," I murmur, capturing her lips in a heated kiss.

"So good..."

Thank God!

Slowly, I stroke deeper, letting her get accustomed to our connection until we find a steady rhythm. Bree's hips lift to meet mine and I smile at the perfection.

With one hand gripping the back of her neck, my other is free to roam her smooth skin and I take full advantage, touching anything within reach. Bree's gasps and little purrs of pleasure guide me, fueling the fire between us. Before I'm ready, my balls tingle, tightening into my body, and like a madman I pump harder, bottoming out with a growl on every stroke.

"Shit, Bree! I'm not going to last." She moans, her walls tightening around me. "Shit! Shit! Shit!"

Frantic, I reach between us, finding that sensitive nub as I lock her to me in a violent kiss. She screams, but I swallow the sound as her orgasm triggers mine, and we fly over the cliff together.

Minutes stretch in the quiet of my master bedroom, only broken by our panting breaths. Flutters tease my softening cock, demanding me to stay in her warmth. "I don't want to leave," I say, working down the length of her neck.

She hums, stroking her fingers through my hair as her body shakes with silent laughter. "I think eventually we'll need food."

"Touche." I pull out, disposing of the condom in a tissue beside the bed. "Would you like a midnight snack?"

"That would require moving."

The knot in my chest loosens at the lightness in her voice. Part of me expected Bree to run after orgasm number one. And after such an amazing time together, that would be awful. Not to mention awkward working together.

Before things get weird, I tug Bree onto my chest, just in case she tries to fly out of my bed. I breathe in the sugary scent of her shampoo and chuckle. "Even your hair smells like a sweet treat, sugar."

Her soft exhale puffs my chest hair as buries her face, laughing. Her fingers stroke my pecs, trailing occasionally to the six-pack I work harder to keep every damn year. I should excuse myself to the restroom, or offer it to Bree, but I can't bear to break the peace of holding her in my arms.

We were in a different world tonight. Away from our roles in the kitchen. And I'm not ready for it to end yet. I feel relaxed for the first time since my business became the sole focus of my life. I'm starting to see how unsatisfying that is when I walk into my lonely house every night.

"I should probably go," she says, startling me out of my rabbit hole of what ifs.

My arm squeezes her shoulder. "Not yet. Rest. I'll make you breakfast in the morning."

The idea flutters excitement in my stomach. It's been ages since I let a woman spend the night. Most angled for it and I wouldn't even bring them back to my place. Now, this little spitfire is angling to escape before my heart rate calms.

Quietness overtakes the room until I realize her breathing has evened out. Without thinking twice, I let the what ifs go and enjoy following Bree into a calm, dreamless sleep.

Sunlight sears through my eyelids, and I groan, dragging the pillow over my face. "Ugh!" I forgot to close the blinds last night.

Shit! Bree!

Throwing my pillow to the floor, I realize my bed is empty, her side cold to the touch, and I jump out of bed, sliding on the pair of boxers I ditched last night. I take the stairs two at a time, listening for any sign of life. I drove the woman here. Certainly, she didn't freak out so much that she'd walk-of-shame into town. The last thing I want is Bree feeling shame or regret this morning.

Finally, the sound of my coffeemaker gurgling gives me hope as I turn the corner into the kitchen. Bree's fantastic ass stands at my range, clad in her tank top and tiny panties she wore underneath her chef's clothes. The caveman part of me wishes I found her in one of my t-shirts, but my cock is more than happy with all the skin on display.

"Morning…"

She jumps, grasping her chest with a squeak. "You scared the crap out of me."

I laugh. "Let's hope not."

"Har, har," she says, rolling her eyes.

Grinning, I slide in behind Bree and wrap my arms around her waist. "What can I say? You bring out the kid in me."

My smart mouth earns me an elbow to the ribs, making me laugh harder. "Alright, old man." The smile that she fires over her shoulder hits me straight in the gut, harder than her cheap shot did, and I growl, trapping my little vixen against the counter.

The coffee maker beeps the end of its cycle, filling the space with a hefty dose of caffeinated cinnamon. "Smells delicious. What did you do to my coffee?" I ask, tracing the curve of her shoulder the way I want to do with my lips.

"Bree's secret sauce. I live off caffeine. I need quality."

"By all means. How do you take it?"

"Black is fine. I like the hit."

Smiling, I pour us both cups and carry them to my breakfast bar, laying out placemats and napkins. "You know, my plan was to cook you breakfast. Not the other way around."

She shrugs. "I couldn't sleep. Hope you don't mind."

The idea of her not sleeping well bothers me, but I try not to let it show and rely on the humor that works for us in the kitchen. "Guess next time I need to wear you out more."

"Next time?" she squeaks, turning with her frittata pan. A sweet blush colors her cheeks, warming my insides.

I bend down and take the pan, capturing her lips with a sigh. "Yes, next time. If you'll have me."

She dips her head, pulling away before I get the answer I'm looking for. Grabbing a mitt, she eases a fresh pan of flaky croissants from the oven, and my mouth drops.

"Holy hell! How long have you been up?"

Waving me off, she acts like fresh baked goods in the morning is nothing. "You have an amazing stash here. I couldn't help myself."

I hold up my hands. "Don't let me stop you. I could get used to waking up like this."

Her face turns an alarming shade of red as she clears her throat. "I explored your garden a bit this morning." A far away daze darkens her eyes. "I always wanted a space like that when I was a kid. Pretty flowers for the table. A swing to read books in. Herbs and vegetables... well, as a kid I wanted fruit and a snickers bush, but still." She grins and I'm taken by her realness. Nothing about Bree is artificial, even on a first date, or first whatever this is.

I grab her elbow, bringing the infuriating woman to sit at the bar instead of waiting on me in my own kitchen. "Sit. I got the rest."

Folding her hands in her lap, Bree looks at me with a little of that sass back. "You mean after I got everything ready?"

"Grr... woman. Are we going to battle over my kitchen?" I move to the fridge. "Would you like some juice? Milk?" I turn, catching her eye. "Mimosa?"

She smirks. "Water is fine."

I grab a bottle and return to sit beside my breakfast partner. "Thank you for cooking." I cut a massive slice of the frittata, serving Bree before myself. "So, what's on tap for today?"

"Oh..." She drops her fork. "I checked out the calendar you sent and knocked out the distillery party coming up. I've got notes to type in your system, but yesterday got away from me."

Holy hell! "Is that why you were late?" Her I-told-you-so stare hits me hard. "Okay. Okay. I get it." Relief is real and alive in my head,

Bree tucks her leg underneath her, looking pleased as punch as she forks a bite of fluffy egg into her mouth. "Their party is going to be awesome, and I think you're going to love the menu suggestions."

"Nice. They're bringing the bottles, right?"

"Yes, and oh my gawd, I am off the bourbon for quite a while."

Our laughter mingles together, lightening the conversation as we dig into breakfast. Almost like a first date, except we slept together last night. And Bree tucking her naked thigh up against her chest only reminds me of those sweet thighs wrapped around my head.

Jesus! I should have slipped on some shorts before I came down this morning, but I was too afraid Bree had run.

Turning toward the counter, I attempt to adjust discreetly, but Bree catches me and shoves my shoulder.

"Pig!"

Grinning, I pull her head in, capturing that upturned pout in a kiss. "Get used to it, sugar. You ripped the Band-Aid off and now I don't think I can go back to not touching you."

"Unc!" Tyler's voice rings through the space as my front door slams.

"Shit!" Hopping up from the chair, I rush to the kitchen doorway, attempting to block Tyler from finding Bree in her underwear in my kitchen.

"Unc!" He comes to a screeching halt at the doorway before I can get there and I slide in front of Bree, attempting to block her while still in my boxers.

Well, that solved the hard on problem.

"Oh, crap... sorry." Tyler turns his back out of respect. *Good boy.* "Yeah, uh... I'll meet ya out front, Unc."

"Right. Be out in a few."

Turning, I bend over Bree's hunched form and kiss her flushed cheek. She seems tucked into herself, which I pray is nothing but attempting to hide her nakedness.

"Are you okay?"

"Sure. Yeah..." She glances toward the door where Tyler disappeared. "Little embarrassing to be caught in her house in my undies, but you know... Go ahead. Do what you gotta do."

I pause at the forced smile Bree plastered on her face, but knowing nothing will be solved with Tyler in the other room, I drop a kiss on the top of her head. "I'll be back in a few. Make yourself at home."

Leaving an uncomfortable Bree sitting in my kitchen tears me apart, but I rush up the stairs for my shorts, and meet my grinning nephew on the front porch in one of the rocking chairs he loved since he was a kid.

"Sorry, Unc. Didn't mean to interrupt."

I snort. "No problem, kid. You got the day off?"

"Nah, just finished up at Smith's and running some errands before relieving Dad at the store."

"Yeah?"

Tyler's nerves are obvious. His rocking is slightly manic. His thumbs tapping on his thighs in between, rubbing his palms down his thighs. Curious, I settle in the chair beside him and smile at the familiarity. We haven't sat like this since the days he was fresh out of the military and dealing with losses only a brother-in-arms would understand. In those times, we had many, many conversations on this porch.

"So, what can I do for ya, Ty?"

His tan face lights up. "I'm going to propose, man."

"What! Wow!" I clap him on the back. "Congratulations, kid!"

He chuckles. "Not congratulations, yet. She still needs to say yes."

"*Hah!* Of course she will. I've seen how you guys look at each other. When you going to do it?"

Tyler's face brightens. "Some of that depends on other people. I designed her ring in Lexington, so waiting on that for one." He leans his head back in the chair and looks at me. "I was hoping I could use the rooftop when it gets done. Maybe have my favorite uncle cook my girl a world class meal."

Pride swells in my chest for this kid. "Count on it! I got you, Ty. Just let me know when and get your ass cooking on that rooftop, cause I've got a party up there in a few weeks as well."

My head is buzzing when we stand up and slap each other on the back with a hug. "I'm happy for you, Tyler. Truly. We'll come up with something great. No worries."

When he pulls back and grasps my hand, his eyes are shining. "Thanks, Unc. For everything." Finally, he tilts his head toward the house with a smirk. "So, what's up in there?"

"Uh uh... not happening." With a grin, I shove my nephew's shoulder toward the steps. "Get your ass to work and tell the old man I said hi."

"Will do, Unc," he says, laughing all the way to the truck.

His hand tosses a wave goodbye, and I turn toward the house, torn between happiness for my nephew and jealousy because he has it all figured out.

Chapter Nine

Bree

It's been two weeks since my night at Tucker's, and not a lot has changed. We haven't had a single moment to ourselves, nor any repeat performance of that night. And my god... my body is craving a repeat of that night.

We've been crazed in the kitchen with parties and receptions. Smith has been all but AWOL, putting the final touches on his bistro, due to open next week. Mark is working our booth at the festival, mainly because Tucker can't trust the new guy on his own. He keeps a pretty heavy eye on him during dinner service.

I was in the kitchen early this morning, prepping tray after tray of treats for the fair. *Two Fourteen* doesn't necessarily need publicity anymore, but every business in the community pitches in for all these town events, so whatever. I'll do my part, as well.

Mark was incredibly thankful for his replenished stock when I dropped fresh desserts while ago. There was a line waiting, but the high schooler Tucker hired to run the cash box is keeping up with the chaos. It's going to be a success for the restaurant's bottom line if we can keep up with production this weekend.

That's a big *if*.

As I make my way through the crowd, toward the restaurant, my mind trips over all the things I need to finish up before doors open. Fall decorations litter the picture windows I pass. Pumpkins, hay bales, and baskets of gourds line the sidewalk. Families are everywhere I look, waiting for the petting zoo, in line for candy and the corn maze.

It's anarchy to my eardrums and I'm itching to get back into my safe space and away from the teeny-tiny munchkins.

Tucker is taking on Tyler's dinner and giving Neil a bigger responsibility for service. A level of nerves sits in my stomach over that, but I need to finish the chocolate ball that will reveal Tyler's engagement ring after we pour the warm caramel bourbon on top. When I suggested the surprise reveal, Tyler flew over the moon.

Construction crews finished upstairs yesterday, and I know he's been in and out all-day decorating. Seems fitting that the inaugural use of the new space will be a proposal. Fits the theme of this town, I guess.

When I reach our alleyway, I hesitate. Neil is out back having a cigarette. I cringe, loathing the idea of walking through his haze of smoke with no one else around. To go in the front door requires walking around the block to the front door, and the idea of dealing with that crowd isn't too appealing either.

Going for the quickest route, I hurry down the alley toward our metal security door, fishing out my badge as I walk.

"Hey, Pinky. Just the woman I wanted to see. Where'd you scurry off to?"

I scowl. I hate that nickname. "Just because my hair is pink, Neil... I have a name."

He sneers, pushing off the brick wall and tossing his bud on the street. His steps are lazy but puts his body between me and the door, unfortunately. By the time he's a few feet away, I smell the lingering stench of alcohol under his cigarette smoke. *Great! He's going to be a load of help tonight.*

"What if I wasn't talkin' bout your hair? Does that help?"

Eew. "Gross, Neil. What the hell?"

Moving to step around him, I accidentally knock his shoulder in my rush, and he stumbles. "Shit!" I catch the lanky man around the waist, propping him upright, which, sadly, he misunderstands, and wraps his other arm around my shoulders.

"Aw, yea." Now on firmer feet, Neil presses his crotch into my abdomen and moans, his hot breath steaming my ear.

"Fuck!" I shove. "Get the hell off me!" Only his inebriated state allows me to budge his heavier weight.

"Come on, Bree... the old man isn't around. You don't have to hide your feelings." He steps forward again and I gasp, sliding out of reach. "What the fuck! I see the way you look at me. You can't want those saggy old man balls over this."

Unh! How dare he!

Neil steps forward, but I sidestep and throw a middle finger over my shoulder. My breath is ragged as I hurry for the door, pretending butterflies aren't flying through my chest with the speed of a hurricane. Footsteps echo at my back, but I swipe my card on the reader before Neil catches up.

I need the comfort of people.

Inside, the bright fluorescents offer some relief, but I don't stop. Neil opens the door as I round the corner, drawing my attention as I turn and slam right into a hard mass.

"Umph. What the..." Strong hands wrap my arms, preventing me from hitting the ground. "Bree?" Tucker's deep rumble eases the tension in my muscles, and I straighten, catching the dark glare Tucker sends behind me.

"Bitch," Neil grumbles, striding past.

"What did you say?" Tucker pushes me behind his back, but Neil keeps walking. "Neil..." He glances down at me, his hazel eyes disturbed. "Bree, what happened?"

I swallow. "He's plastered. We had a-a scuffle outside."

"What the fuck does that mean?" His voice rises. And before I can stop him, Tucker takes off down the hallway, me hot on his heels. "Neil, get back here!"

Eyes track our movement. Me tugging at Tucker's arm. Him pressing into the new chef's space with a face redder than I've seen it.

"Tucker, stop. I'm fine."

"You need to explain." He stabs a finger into Neil's chest, growling.

Kelsey, the floor manager, rushes through the swinging doors. "Guys, guys... we can hear y'all out front. What's going on?"

"Kels, I need you to text Smith and Mark. We're going to need backup tonight."

"Fuck you! I'm fine to work," Neil says, stumbling back a step.

"Watch your mouth. You are in no state to work. What the hell were you thinking?" Disappointment slices through the anger in Tucker's voice, and he shakes his head.

Unfortunately, Neil makes the mistake of swinging at Chef's cheek. A long, sloppy drawback that a blind person could see coming. Tucker slides to the side, grabbing Neil's wrist, and putting his face down on the stainless steel with the speed of a young MMA fighter.

"Tuck!" I gasp, jumping out of their way. My heel trips on the edge of a non-skid mat, sending me to my ass beside the men. Embarrassment flames my cheeks, but Kelsey is at my side quick, helping me to my feet and out of the way.

Tucker's worried gaze scans me, head to toe, but he doesn't let go of our wayward chef. He jerks Neil upright, turning him toward the back as the man struggles to keep his feet.

"You need me, you ass." Neil seems to realize he fucked up, but judging from his choice of words, he's not willing—or is too drunk—to swallow his pride.

Tucker's silence says it all as he all but hauls Neil to the back door. Shouted curses fly our way until the slam of metal cuts them off and Chef stalks back to the kitchen, fury practically steaming from his ears. His eyes burn black as they lock on me.

"Whew… damn." Kelsey pats my shoulder as she backs away, leaving me with an overwhelming chef and way too many overwhelming feelings.

"Are you okay?" he asks, stroking under my chin.

To my utter horror, my eyes water, the emotional roller coaster of the last thirty minutes finally crashing.

"Aww, babe." Tucker pulls me into the safety of his arms, and I breathe in his calming scent. "It's okay, now. That dumbass is gone."

Exhaling, I pull back, swiping my bangs from my eyes with a massive amount of relief. "I'm good. I'm good." Tucker smiles at me, shaking my hands and arms, ridding that darkness from my chest. "I hate confrontation. That's all."

Tucker seems to understand that I need space and backs off after a light kiss to my lips. "As long as you're okay." He glances around to our sparse kitchen and curses. "We've got a fuck-ton to do now. Think I could bum your hands on the line tonight?"

Laughing, I shove my boss for the next eight hours toward his apron and snatch my own, getting back to our rolls in the kitchen. "I got you."

Thankfully, Vinny steps into the kitchen after clocking in, followed by Smith, and I breathe a sigh of relief.

"What's going on, old man?" Smith asks, scanning for that missing scab Tucker ripped off. "Kels texted 9-1-1 with just Neil's name."

"He's out," Chef says, slapping his head chef on the back. "I thought you were working your booth tonight."

"S'alright. I left Liza in charge and my dad's hanging out in the tent with her."

"Nice. Well, if you got time, could you take charge of main? I've got a side project and I'll pop in the line when I can."

Smith smirks. "My boy's big night." He whoops loud, his pride and happiness for his friend obvious.

Chef claps, a lightness taking over the kitchen now that the wart has been removed. "Damn straight! Now let's get the hell on with this night. I need a freaking drink already, man."

With that, we all separate to our stations, readying for the evening. Vinny actually steps in to prep the salad station, doing a damn good job of stepping up. For the next few hours, we put our heads down and work. I help with being a runner when needed and fetch things from the pantry in between tickets. The place is mildly chaotic given the business of the festival going on tonight. The crowd rolls in spurts, but about halfway through service, a server runs in to say the terrace is occupied. Code for 'Tyler is in the house'.

"Here we go."

Everyone keeps on our toes, perfecting every plate that leaves the pass. Tyler's dessert is ready to send when we get the word, and thankfully, things are slowing down. I finally feel like I can breathe. Tucker leaves the kitchen with Tyler's starter course. I assume to welcome the happy couple and give his nephew a touch of support.

The rest of the night goes smoothly. The dining room is practically dead. Enough that the servers start their side work, and the kitchen cleans between a random ticket.

Finally, Kelsey comes in personally for Tyler's dessert ball.

Nerves roll through my stomach. "God, I hope he likes the treat."

"I hope she says yes," Tucker jokes, grinning.

Smith smacks him on the back, laughing. "Don't jinx the man." He flips a chicken breast on the grill. "I'm starving guys. Want a sandwich since we're twiddling thumbs here."

Ayes ring across the board and Smith tosses on more buns and breasts for a family dinner after we close up shop.

Tucker takes a moment to visit my station, leaning his hip on the area I was cleaning. "How are you?"

He's unbuttoned his chef jacket, looking like an edible hunk of man with those tight biceps crossed over his chest. It doesn't help that I know exactly how cut that chest is now, exactly how edible the man, and now, I've also seen the sexy protective side willing to jump in a scuffle to defend someone he... cares about.

"I'm good." I shrug. "We survived."

His face twists in disbelief. "But how are *you* doing?"

I smack his stomach. "I'm fine. Really. Now move your butt. I'm ready to get home and crash in my bed."

Tucker doesn't listen. He steps forward instead, crowding my space. "What if you didn't? Come to my place instead."

The huskiness of his voice does something to my stomach, twisting and turning every nerve in my body until I'm biting my tongue to not say something stupid.

Misunderstanding my hesitation, Tucker dips down low, catching my eyes, and he catches my chin. This is the first time he's touched me at work, or in front of other people, and it dawns on me how much I've held back, not wanting to feel like his dirty little secret.

I try to turn my head, checking our audience, but Tucker holds strong. His eyes glimmer in the light, punching me with the emotion buried there. "Look at me, Bree. When Neil came in earlier and I thought he hurt you, I wanted to explode." He swallows, dropping his forehead to mine. "I wanted to kill him and only having you there stopped me."

My hands reach out, steadying myself against the hard body I want to let go with and hold so badly.

"What I realized, though, is I'm tired of this limbo, Bree. I want it all." He pulls back, searching my eyes, and puffs out a heavy breath. "My nephew is grabbing life by the balls tonight, Bree. The boy's putting me to shame."

A laugh slips out. "You're doing pretty good, I'd say. Boss?"

He growls. "Screw the boss shit. Take a chance on me, Bree. I think it'll be worth it. I goddamn do."

I tilt my chin higher, grinning at the growly nature of his voice, the possessiveness. Wrapping my arms around Tucker's neck, I surprise both of us by pulling his head down for a swooping kiss.

"Woo Ooo..." Hollars and claps ring loud through the kitchen when Tucker scoops me up in his arms, capturing my lips and releasing all the stress we've held tonight. "Get it, boss."

He sets me down, our bodies shaking with laughter. The final seeds of doubt wash away, hearing our friends' and coworkers' overwhelming support.

"What do you say?" Tucker asks, grinning against my lips.

Sneakily, I work a hand under the hem of his shirt, stroking over the sexy *v* there. "How soon can we leave?"

"Ugh!" Tucker groans, his stomach twitching under my fingers. When he looks up at the ceiling, I kiss his Adam's apple there.

"Get out of here, kids," Smith calls. "We've got clean up."

Looking around Tucker's shoulder, I smirk at Smith, who winks.

"You heard him," Tucker whispers in my ear.

I shiver. "What are you waiting for?"

Groaning, he grabs my hand and tugs for the exit. But we don't get far. The kitchen door flies open, revealing Tucker's beaming nephew dragging his—I assume—new fiancée behind his back. She's adorable, dressed in a knee-length floral dress, ruffled at the sleeves, and a wide belt that highlights amazing breasts that would cause me to hate her if she didn't look so damn sweet.

And honestly, I've heard her backstory. It's shit. So, I'm happy she found an extremely handsome man happy to sweep her off her feet.

They're both beaming. Tyler tucks his girl under his arm and they both shout out. "We're engaged!"

Rounds of backslapping hugs pass around the men, with softer congratulations to the girl. Tucker holds Tyler close, whispering something in his ear that brings tears to his eyes.

The woman steps to me, her own eyes gleaming. "Your dessert was absolutely beautiful. Thank you so much for making it for us!"

"You're welcome. I'm so happy you liked it. Oomph." She slams into my chest with an excited hug, and I laugh. "Congratulations!" I pat her back a few times until Tyler pulls her away.

"I'm going to go celebrate with my lady. I just wanted to thank you guys for everything."

A chorus of goodbyes and well wishes follow them out, but Tucker already has my elbow and is moving toward the door.

My stomach somersaults with excitement, and nerves, and all kinds of pressure now that our relationship just got outed in spectacular fashion.

Chapter Ten

Tucker

Today marks three weeks since Bree and I went public, and things are about as smooth as they can go between an overly exhausted old man and a vibrant, love-phobic vixen.

I left her in my bed with a note that I was stealing the muffins she baked yesterday for my brother. It's my day off, so I've got a lot to get done, so despite closing late, I was up early for a workout. Jameson mocked the hell out of me when we left the gym for getting with a woman he guarantees will expand my waistline. Then, I made fun of him for worrying about his waistline.

I figure with the amount of acrobatics having a hot woman in my bed inspires, I should be fine.

This morning, I am glad her pastries are impossible to turn down though, because I'm going to use them to bribe my brother. He never turns down carbs.

Parking beside the hardware store, I grab the plastic container of muffins and the French Kiss coffees I picked up on the way over and lock my truck.

This time of day, the only people in the store are the old men my brother hangs out with. Despite being ten years older than me, my brother is a weirdo who has more in common with eighty-year-old cronies than people his own age. He swears they're perfect, because he'll never feel old next to their stiff backs and knee replacements.

At least those old guys won't complain about the interruption.

"Haven't you done enough?"

The raspy voice startles me as I pass the dumpster beside the store, almost upending my treats to the ground.

"What the hell?"

"Real nice, chef. Is Mr. Goody Goody skittish?" A disheveled man stumbles to his feet, and despite the extra length to his hair, his stained clothes, and dirty skin, I'd recognize Neil anywhere.

"Were you sleeping there?"

"What's it to you?" Neil bends over and collects his duffel and a few loose items into a plastic bag. I can't help but notice one is an amber-colored square bottle. "I'm not trespassin'," he says, confident even with his slur.

"Actually, you are." I point at the brick building. "That's my brother's store. Also, why aren't you at Ben's place?"

"Kicked me out. But you know that, don't ya?"

My jaw drops. "The fuck? How would I know that?"

Honestly, I've avoided going to the house because of Neil. Ben has taken to picking up meals instead when he does the drive by of grabbing French Kiss's leftover pastries.

"Don't lie about that shit. You fired me and told the old bastard to kick me out." His arm swings wide, giving me the wide view of his apparent bedroom before he steps forward, scowling. "All this shit is your fault." He shoves at my chest. "Does it make you feel like a big man, controlling all our lives like that? I piss off your little princess and you go cave man and get me kicked out of my house."

Lifting my hands, I try to ease the cornered pit-bull look in Neil's eye. "I didn't at all get you kicked out. This is the first I'm hearing of it. But Neil, Ben is a fair man... if something happened..." I leave the sentence hanging, knowing completely that thought will set all kinds of crazy off in the man.

"Fuck you, *chef*," he drawls, sarcasm dripping from the moniker. He starts walking backwards, toward main street, sneering at me the whole way. "One day, old man. Someone's going to teach you what it's like to lose."

With that eerie sentiment, Neil turns and disappears, leaving me unsettled, holding a silly bribe on the side of my brother's store. The goddamn sun has barely peeked over the horizon and my stomach is in knots already.

Inside the store, I try to shake off my melancholy and deal with the job ahead. As is his routine, my brother is in the back of the store, leading point with the town's elder crew, teaching them how to build a bird feeder. Those old men don't look strong enough to hold a hammer, but that's not stopping a one of them.

"I should have brought more coffee," I say, striding through their circle.

"Gents, say hi to my talented brother, but don't stop sanding. We're going to get this feeder together today come hell or high water."

Waving, I move to slap my brother's back and drop his breakfast. "Ahh, baked goods." He shoots a knowing look at the gentlemen. "That means, my dear, baby brother wants something."

"Shush. I bring you food all the time."

Laughter rattles around the class, the men offering bribes to take my brother's muffin off his hands. "I promise, gentlemen, next time I'll bring more." Turning to my brother, I lower my voice. "Can we chat a minute?"

He smirks. "Sure thing, Tuck." He wipes his hands, leaving instruction for the men's next step before stepping into the back office with me.

"First... did you know there was a man sleeping beside the dumpster outside?"

My brother starts. "No! What the hell?"

I nod. "Yeah. An ex-employee and he's not looking well."

"I'll keep an eye. Does he need help?"

Looking to the ceiling, I pray for patience to control the vitriol wanting to come out of my mouth. "Let's just say that help was freely offered, taken up on, and discarded quicker than last week's trash."

"Okay. I got it. I'll keep an eye, though." He eyes me. "What else ya need, brother?"

"*Hah!* Straight to the point. I need a few things, actually. I need to borrow your truck for one. There's a swing in Lex that Bree would love in the garden. They're holding it for me, but I really need to pick it up today and it won't fit in my SUV."

He nods. "No problem, man. You know that."

"Yeah, thanks though. I'm going to get with Tyler about adding onto my garage as well."

"Need extra space for another car?" My brother wiggles his bushy eyebrows, reminding me of when I told him about my first kiss.

"What are you, twelve?"

His mustache twitches as he digs into his desk drawers and tosses me the leather strap that holds his truck keys. "I'd offer to go help you schlep the thing back, but you know... old men with hammers... gotta save these guns for the hard work." He strains a surprisingly fit bicep, and I shake my head.

"Excuses. Excuses. But thanks, man."

He stands, giving me a brotherly hug as he walks me out. "I'm happy for you, Tuck."

I say my goodbye and head for my brother's truck, the stress I walked in with completely forgotten. The day ahead and the weekend ahead are going to be nuts. Maybe I should have picked a calmer time to make these changes, but when is anything easy?

Having Bree waking up most mornings in my bed has kicked ideas for the future in high gear. It's made me realize how unsatisfied I've been lately with the bachelor lifestyle. A quiet house. Working nonstop. What's the point when there's no one to enjoy the fruits of my labor with?

As I pull out of the hardware shop, I scan the streets for any sight of Neil, wondering if I should call Ben and update him on our friend. We've had veterans who were hard to help before.

Unfortunately, we can't force someone to choose a certain path. And it's not something I can worry about today.

It's mid-afternoon before I've finished setting up Bree's surprise. The swing fit perfect on the edge of the garden, shaded from the afternoon sun by the trees rimming the fence. I moved a few planters by the sides to give the illusion of blending in with nature. From here, I have a full view of the garden and all the fresh floral smells that come with it.

It's peaceful. Which I need with my stomach twisted with nerves.

I've been careful to not push too fast, knowing Bree's skittish of relationships. Given the way she grew up, I'm not surprised. Foster kids don't always get the care and understanding they need. Let alone love. But there's no doubt, that's where my feelings are.

Before I laid a finger on her, I knew my girl was special. Now that I've spent over a year getting to know her, working with her, and almost a month seeing her gorgeous face at my side, day in day out, there's no denying.

Smoothing a hand down my chest, I straighten the wrinkles out of the button down I put on after my shower. I thought about a jacket, but Bree would know something was up then and I just want her relaxed for what I want to ask her, what I want to tell her. I set up a bucket with a chilled Chardonnay, and a plate of nibbles. A blanket. Pillows. All that's missing is Bree.

No sooner do I start doubting my timing than I hear Bree's little hatchback pull down the drive. I hate that car. It's way too likely to breakdown, but that's another thing to deal with down the road.

For now, I stand, catching her attention with a wave. Bree's mouth falls open, her eyes bright and shining with happiness.

"What is this?"

Grinning, I hold out my hand, which she walks over to take, eyeing the swing behind me.

"This is beautiful. Where did you find it?"

"Been searching for a while. Found it online, over in Lexington."

She beams, her cheeks turning a rosy pink as I guide her to sit, bringing her legs into my lap and covering them with a blanket.

"Wow!" she says as I hand her a glass of her favorite wine. That tiny pink tongue darts out to wet her lips, and I can't resist. I capture a taste of her own sweetness before it gets tainted with tart grapes.

We clink glasses before I snuggle her into my chest, rubbing her calves as she leans her head in.

"How was the kitchen? Did you get what you wanted done?"

She sighs. "Mostly. Part needs to wait until tomorrow, but I got everything prepped ahead that I could. I'll head in early and knock the rest out."

I squeeze her shoulder, loving my girl's work ethic and care for my restaurant. "I'll hit the farmer's market first thing in the morning," I say, fighting the guilt trying to work its way in for not working right now. "This is the biggest party we've hosted in house while the restaurant was open. I've got to get off my ass and hire a few more chefs. We can't keep killing ourselves with these hours."

She pats my chest, leaning up to drop a chaste kiss under my jaw, and my cock jerks. "We'll get it done. Don't worry."

Needing her closer, I tug Bree into my lap and she squeals, almost toppling her wine in my lap. "Thank you," I say, resting my head against her hair.

"For what? I should thank you for this setup. This is amazing."

Her warmth snuggled into my chest in the cool fall afternoon is my picture of heaven. "I'm glad you like it. You've been working so hard for the restaurant, I wanted to do something for you."

Tilting her chin, I dive into those lips that drive me wild, swallowing our passion with a moan. I place my glass on the side table with Bree's so I can turn her in my lap. She straddles my waist, her tiny hands diving in my hair and giving as good as she gets. Her hips dip against my straining erection, riding sensuously until I can't take the pain anymore.

"Off!" Grabbing her waistband, I tug, needing access to her silky wetness. Pre-cum leaks as I watch her hop up and scan our location as she drops her pants. "No one can see us back here."

To prove my point, I loosen my belt and slide my jeans and boxers down as well.

She shoves my shoulders before I get them off my ankles and I crash back to the swing, our laughter filling the afternoon. Never have I laughed with a woman during sex. It's never felt this crazed with just one touch.

Without wasting a second, Bree climbs in my lap, wrapping the blanket around her shoulders to hide her bare backside. My arms slide up her back, holding her tight against my chest as she slides that wetness down my cock, sheathing me in her velvety softness.

"God, Bree!"

"So good..." she gasps as I pulse my hips, angling myself deeper. "Tuck!"

Our connection builds slowly, Bree's hips curling in decadent strokes, taking our emotions flying with our hormones. My heart pounds in my chest, needing to be closer, needing to climb inside this woman and never leave.

Our lips hover a breath apart, sharing each other's air as we ride the waves of pleasure. "Bree!" Her name is a prayer, the feelings becoming too much. My hands grip the back of her head, holding her to me. "Open your eyes."

They fly open and I see exactly what I need mirrored.

"Bree, I love you."

She gasps, her green eyes watering as she smiles, kissing the words right off my lips as she flies over the cliff. Her muscles tighten, milking me over the edge with her with a shout. Pulse after pulse coat her insides, bare for the first time.

We didn't even discuss it, but feeling our wetness mingle together, dripping back onto my thighs, brings out a caveman in me I didn't know existed.

That part is satisfied to sit outside with Bree's arms locked around my neck, her panting breath slowly returning to normal.

The more civilized part knows that any one of my neighbors could walk over at anytime, and while we're covered, I wouldn't want any of them seeing my woman vulnerable like this. She's mine.

What do you know... guess both sides are feeling the caveman with Bree.

"What do you say we take this inside?" I whisper, not wanting to disturb our peace. We both have to be up bright and early in the morning. But there's still hours for me to enjoy my woman. Preferably in a bed with room to spread her out and make up for lost time.

There's still a big conversation to be had about her moving in. And after our little time in the swing, hopefully there will be conversation about plans for the future, hopes, dreams... all of it.

Chapter Eleven

Bree

From the moment I woke up this morning, a giddiness settled in my chest, giving me renewed energy to get through this weekend.

There's so much to get done for tonight's party, but Tuck and I making breakfast together before going our separate ways felt so domestic this morning. It has me flying on air. His home is everything I would have picked for myself. A chef's dream, really.

I check my phone. Tucker should be almost done at the farmer's market, and I'm feeling better about having everything ready for tonight.

Slipping my earbuds in, I flip on one of my lighter playlists and lay out the spring pans for my cheesecake. The girls are going to love the bourbon caramel sauce I came up with for their crushed praline cheesecake. Tyler's chocolate bomb dessert inspired the idea. I can't get enough of my new favorite sauce.

My face flushes as I plug in the mixer. Maybe I'll take home the leftovers and surprise Tucker with some special fun.

I don't think he'll complain if he finds me naked in his bed, covered with this crack sauce. At least I hope he doesn't. It could get sticky, but damn. I lick some of the caramelized sugar from my finger and bite back a moan.

Yeah, that's going to be fun later.

Chuckling, I head to the pantry for the nuts I need to crush. Admittedly, there's an extra bounce in my step and I'm not mad about it. Tucker and I taking our relationship to a new level has given me more peace than I thought possible. From the little, unloved girl in foster care, to a partner for one of the most gorgeous, protective, top-class chefs I know.

It's scary, because my heart is on the line. For the first time ever.

Last night, when Tucker laid his feelings on the table, I should have confided in him then, but I panicked. To his credit, he didn't push, and he didn't get upset or hurt. I guess that's the benefit of relationships with older men. They are confident in who they are and what they want.

That he's confident in the sack and more than willing to pleasure me... repeatedly... is like the best caramel icing on a cake.

Giggling, I head to the back of the room, stacking flour, sugar, pecans, and pralines in my arm. My hips bounce to the beat in my ears as I scan for anything else I need. Not that I could carry anymore. My arms are overflowing.

Two trips then.

Turning for the door, I frown that it slammed shut behind me. We usually leave the thing open for easy access.

"Shit." I lean my weight against the metal, hoping it gives easily. It doesn't. "Come on." I shift the stuff in my arms, trying to slip the handle with my elbow. Not an inch.

Stepping back, I balance on one leg and try to press with my foot instead. I need more leverage. I stare at the lever. *What the hell?*

"Fine." Sitting my stuff down, I lean on the handle with both hands. Why won't this damn thing budge?

Frustrated, I kick at the bottom of the door, jigging the stuck handle back and forth with all the weight I can muster. "Come on, you little shit!"

Huffing, I lean my back against the door, dropping my head to the metal. My eyes scan the room, searching for something I can use to pry the handle. Thankfully, nothing is waiting for me in the oven, but that doesn't mean I want to camp out in here until the rest of the staff come in.

A massive serving spoon in one of the bins looks promising. I snatch it and try to shove the edge under the plate hiding the screws. The silver scratches metal, leaving marks I'll have to explain later. But it still doesn't give. "Come on!" I scream, slamming my palm to the door.

Needing a moment to thank, I squat into a seated position, dropping my head in my hands. My phone is on the table out there. No one is expected for hours. That takes away all the time I've made up today. No way will Tucker and I have time for nakey play. *Ugh!*

I know it's stupid to be disappointed, but I am.

Staring at the door, my brain stumbles through what is left to do. It won't be impossible if I get out of here in the next hour or so. My stupid, stupid luck.

As I'm kicking myself, a shadow passes underneath the crack of the door and I jump up. "Hello! Hello!" My fist slams the door, making as much noise as possible. "Is someone there? Hello!"

Not a sound. Did my eyes play tricks on me?

"Hello!"

The scent of smoke wafts under the door. *Is someone cooking? That doesn't smell like the grill.*

"Tucker?"

No response. I try the handle again, and it's warmer to the touch. I jerk my hand away. "Shit!"

Dragging in a deep breath, I shove down the panic. "What do I do? What do I do?" I mumble, looking around the room. It's cinderblock. No windows. No fire extinguisher.

How is there smoke? I left nothing in the oven. I swear.

Immediately, my thoughts drift to Tucker. This place is his baby. We can't lose it.

"Help! Help!" I scream at the top of my lungs, banging the door repeatedly.

The smoke floating harder under the door gets thicker, reeking of charred lumber. That gives me pause. Almost the entire kitchen is metal or ceramic. Only the tables and floors in the dining room are wood. Is the fire that large already?

Oh my god!

Panic rises in my chest, hard and fast, stealing the air from my lungs. I move away from the door and the billowing smoke, searching for anything to plug the hole. My hand towel is at my station. Unless I can shove bushels of carrots under the door, there's not a lot that will fit.

Tossing stuff off the shelf, I finally find some butcher paper and pull it off the cardboard. Not very fire-retardant, but maybe it'll slow the smoke. I just need enough time for someone to notice the smoke and call the fire department. Crumpling the material, I tuck it in the crease, coughing as the smoke nails me in the face.

My eyes water as I back up, watching the pitiful excuse for protection. All I can do is wait. I drop to the floor, wrapping my arms around my knees, and cover my mouth with my shirt.

Tears spill over as regrets push to the surface. It's the first time I've cried in maybe ten years. Things felt so good. An hour ago, I had so much time, so many feelings to explore. I should have told Tucker how I felt last night. A barrage of all the happy moments, all the sweet touches, collide now that I'm facing the end.

What if no one finds me?

Sobs wrack my body as I try to send a mental message to Tucker. He needs to know I love him if this is it. His name chants over and over in my head. Finally, I curl into a ball and hug myself, waiting for a sign as I watch more and more noxious fumes steal the breathable air.

Chapter Twelve

Tucker

My cell rings in my pocket, vibrating against my thigh, and I sigh. The elderly lady in front of me is taking forever to pay, using her time to catch up on the matchmaking efforts around town.

I roll my eyes at the two of them.

Impatiently, I shift my feet, eyeing the box of purchased supplies on the ground. The load of squash in my arms is getting heavy, but after I check out, I only need to visit two more vendors. It's been a productive morning. I'm just happy I'm almost done.

There's a chill in the air proving that fall is in full swing. Maybe an extra stop for coffee will settle the rocks sitting in my gut. I feel off-kilter. Like a storm cloud is waiting to roll in and ruin my happiness.

Last night was perfect, short of hearing those three little words back from my vixen. Her eyes say she feels it, so I'm okay with waiting. We still got ready together this morning with a plan for the day, even going our separate ways. It was all very domestic. Something I never saw myself getting at my age.

"Alright, love. You have a wonderful day spoilin' those grand-babies."

Fuckin' finally!

"Bye, now."

Smiling, I nod at the woman walking away, looking like she wants to stop for another chat. *My arms are full lady.*

Before she can strike up a conversation, I drop my load on the table and pull out my wallet. My phone vibrates again, and this time I check the number. It's a local area code. I frown, setting my phone down to finish checking out.

"Thank you so much," I say, adding the squash to my basket. I prop the basket on my hip and head for the last booth, only to have my phone immediately vibrate again.

"Shit." I tug it out of my pocket. Same number. I hit the green button. "Hello..."

In my ear, sirens and shouting voices stop me cold. "Mr. Jackson?" All the blood drains from my face, my ears roaring with a sense of foreboding. "Tucker?"

"Uh, yeah. What's going on?"

"This is Kip, the fire chief with KSFD. We received a call about smoke billowing from the back of your restaurant."

I gasp, dropping my crate on the ground to run faster. Confused shoppers eye me as I race past. Kip is talking in my ear, explaining the sight they found when they arrived. His voice is nothing but a blur until one question cuts through my fog.

"Your restaurant is closed this early in the morning. Correct? The boys have the fire under control. We're going to sweep for hot spots, but I wanted to confirm that there should be no sign of life at this hour."

My head swims and I stop, dropping my hands to my knees to suck in a breath. A cold sweat breaks out down my back as my vision narrows and I fight blacking out.

"Bree... Bree is in there. Kitchen," I say, my voice hoarse. I close my eyes, willing the tears to clear as I take off running. No way am I losing her now. The restaurant can burn to ash, but she won't go down with it.

"Shit! Going in! Hunter! Kitchen!"

I hang up on the chief, hauling ass to get to my car, and to my girl. On the way, I call Smith and let him know what's going on. There's nothing the kid can do that the firefighters aren't, but I feel like I need someone who understands there. Someone to take care of the restaurant shit, because my focus is getting to Bree.

Every finger, toe, and hair is crossed on my body that she didn't show up, or maybe she finished early and left.

A whole myriad of what-ifs roll through my head as I speed an arrest-level speed through town. My chest feels too tight, my skin itchy, giving me flashbacks to feelings I've long buried. It's been over a decade since I've seen a war zone, but the panic inside me feels the exact same.

By the time I pull in front of the restaurant, the firefighters have blocked off the parking lot. I get it, but the anxiety is ripping me apart. I need to get to her.

Parking down the street only spikes my heart rate higher. It's farther to run. Longer until I see her pretty face standing perfectly happy and healthy, if I'm sure a little worried outside of the fire. I need to see her safe.

My boots hit the pavement, vibrating my knees with every jarring step. Halfway down the block, Tyler's face comes into view. He's running from his truck at the other end of the block.

"Unc! Unc!"

I throw up my hand, happy to have another set of hands I trust at my side, but I can't stop. My focus is on that front door. Firefighters have their water hose hooked to the fire hydrant out front and are dousing the rooftop and the rear of the building. The kitchen.

Blockades hold onlookers back across the street, but I don't spare them more than a second glance. A hunched figure in a baseball cap hovers alone in the back row, seeming out of place with the concerned shop owners all hugging each other and whispering.

I can't focus on that. Tyler yells my name, but I know if he catches up, he'll try to talk to me out of this. Before he gets close enough, I beeline for the door. Outwardly, there are less signs of fire there. And I'm the one who knows where her station is, not the firefighters.

One of the uniformed men rushes my way, but I'm through the door, coughing immediately when an enormous cloud of smoke smacks me in the face. I drop, using the few feet of clearance at the floor to get my bearings.

"Wha the fud you doin'?" A masked face appears at my shoulder, jerking my weight backwards.

"Get off!" I cough, shoving at his massive, turnout-covered chest. "Gotta... Get my girl." A fit of coughs cut off my sentence, giving the guy the leverage to drag me backwards.

My eyes burn like mad, but I blink, attempting to clear the pain to scan the dining room. Just then, the doorway to the kitchen knocks open. Another burly fireman fills the space, turning sideways to fit through the tight space with the cargo hanging from his arms. My precious cargo.

The guy holding my elbow stops me from rushing forward. "Go! Go! Go!"

All three of us—four of us—fall into the fresh morning air. My knees hit the concrete outside for a split second before the oaf on my arm drags the farther away. A man who is obviously the chief pushes through the chaos.

"What the fuck were you thinking?" he shouts. "You could have been killed. My *men* could have been killed looking for you."

"Sorry," I grumble, shoving around his shoulder toward the other firefighter, who lays Bree on a waiting stretcher behind an ambulance. My heart sinks at her floppy arms and dead weight. She looks so fragile passed out on the tiny bed.

"Bree! Baby!" My eyes scan her body, afraid to touch in case she's burned or injured somewhere.

A Paramedic fits an oxygen mask over her face, smearing the soot streaking her perfect skin. "Are you family?" she asks, checking Bree's vitals.

"Yes. Yes, I am." *I'm hoping to be.*

"We're going to take her in. Would you like to ride in the back?" She glances at my frazzled state. "Actually, sir, we can check you out as well."

I shake her off before she tries to get me to sit. "You take care of her. I'm fine."

Tyler comes up behind me and pulls me into a bear hug. "What were you thinking, Unc? You could have died in there!"

His squeeze sets loose a series of coughs that have the paramedic reaching for another oxygen mask. I take it, just to get her attention off me and where it belongs.

Satisfied, the paramedics strap Bree to the table and load her into the back of the van.

"How is she?" Tyler's somber voice cracks and I shake my head.

"I-I don't know." I glance at my nephew, at the worry wrinkling his brow. "Thank you for being here, Ty." My smoldering restaurant is a mess behind us, but all I can do is pray for minimum damage. The paramedics give me the signal and I hug Tyler, giving him a slap to the back. More for my benefit than anything. "Look, Smith should be on his way. I... I've got to go with her."

"He texted me. Don't worry, Unc. We've got this. You take care of your girl."

Nodding, I swallow past the lump in my throat. "Thanks, kid. Love you."

With that, I climb into the back of the ambulance, out of the medic's way. Bree's chest moving up and down with her breathing is my only comfort with the stench of smoke and char filling the space. They attach monitors and an IV to my girl while I watch. The steady beep-beep of her heart soothes my soul as I try to forget the scene we're leaving behind.

Chapter Thirteen

Bree

A dark peace surrounds me as my body floats on a pillowy cloud. My arms and legs won't move. They're too heavy, as if I'm sinking under a calm lagoon.

In the distance, an annoying bird chirps, pulling me out of my sleep. It's loud and annoying, chirping over and over, the steady rhythm driving me crazy.

Fine!

Lifting my eyelids is a battle. *I'm so tired.*

Finally, they crack open, and I blink. *The sun is so bright in here... what the hell?*

"Bree... Bree, baby. Come back to me."

I close my eyes to the light, groaning at the glow penetrating my lids.

"Bree?" Tucker's sweet voice calls me back to reality.

I peek through the glare to find those soft hazel eyes inches from my face. "Hi..." My voice is barely audible, and Tucker frowns. An elephant sits on my chest, making every breath feel like breathing through a straw.

"Nurse!" His shout echoes to the doorway and through my head. I cringe. "Sorry, baby." He lowers his voice and leans over my bed. "How are you feeling?"

"Thirsty." My lip cracks when I try to talk, and Tucker reaches over to the side table beside the bed and grabs a yellow container. He opens it and rubs a light coating of Vaseline on my lips. "Thank you," I say, blinking away tears.

No one has ever taken care of me like this... ever.

Tucker presses the call button and wraps my free hand in his, squeezing it to his lips. "I'm so happy you're awake, Bree. You scared the hell out of me."

"You look exhausted," I say, stroking the frown drawing those sexy lips downward. Tucker's haggard appearance floors me. His dirty blond hair is wild on top, as if his fingers have been running the lengths. Those bloodshot eyes have large purple bags underneath.

"It's been a hell of a few days."

"Days?" No wonder the IV in my arm itches as bad as this scratchy hospital gown. And it's clear that's where I am. "What about the party? Were the girls disappointed?"

Tucker nods, squeezing his eyes shut. "They understood. Everyone sends you well wishes. They're going to wait until we back up and running to have their party."

My lip quivers at their sweetness.

Memories flood to the surface, fear and pain swilling around my head as reality crashes around me. The fire. Being trapped. Screaming and calling for help. And then the heat. That inferno threatening right outside the pantry I was trapped in.

The last thing I remember is wishing I had confided my feelings to Tucker when I had the chance.

"Tucker, I—"

"Good morning, sleepyhead. Someone's finally awake." An overly cheerful nurse makes her way inside my room, moving to the machine monitoring my heart rate. She scribbles something on the pad in front of her and attaches a blood pressure cuff to my arm. "How are you feeling?"

Tucker speaks up, which I'm thankful for since every word drags nails up my windpipe. "Her mouth and throat are dry. Can someone grab her a water, or juice, or something?"

"I'll grab some ice chips until the doctor gets into see her." That semi-relaxes Tucker, who sits back in the vacant chair at my side and lays his head in my lap. The nurse leaves, winking an exaggerated wink on her way out the door.

"You should probably go home and get some sleep, Tuck."

"Not while you're here. Not leaving." Those strong arms circle my hips, hugging me tight as I stroke his hair, running the softness through my fingers, scratching the rough buzz at the sides peppered with a dusting of salt. It's barely noticeable but only increases the man's sexiness. His face is just beautiful.

"Need a haircut," he mumbles against my stomach.

I chuckle. "I'll do it for you."

"Thanks, baby." Tucker's voice trails off before the nurse returns with the chips, his lips parting on a soft snore.

My fingers never stop moving, soothing myself with the contact. The freedom to touch this sexy man, the ability to.

"I love you, Tucker."

Overcome with exhaustion, I lean my head back and let sleep take me. This time, fully and utterly relaxed.

"When can I leave?" I ask, practically stomping like an irritated toddler.

Tucker smiles indulgently and takes my purse from my hand. Sitting it on the bed, he strides over until we stand toe to toe. My arms crossed to his, loosely resting on my shoulders.

I throw my arms wide. "I'm dressed. They gave me the go ahead and now we've waited on stupid paperwork for over an hour?" Tucker chuckles, but bites it off at my glare. The fact that I'm pouting pisses me off, but I can't help it. "I'm just ready to go home."

Thankfully, my tests were all clear after the fire. Just a little smoke inhalation. Turned out getting trapped in the pantry saved me seared skin, or worse. Now, I'm itching to get away from the smell of antiseptic. Some decent food would be nice for a change, too.

Proving my point, my stomach rumbles, loud enough for Tucker to hear. "Is someone hangry?" he asks, and I scowl.

"Not funny, mister. I will be a lot happier after a cheeseburger and my own bed."

My words toss a bucket of ice water on Tucker's bright mood. He sighs, tugging my hand until we sit on the stiff floral couch along the wall. "I wanted to talk to you about that."

"Did something happen?" Images of my apartment on fire flash like a movie reel in my head. "Did Neil do something else?"

Tucker explained everything the fire inspector found during their investigation. Smith led the charge while Tucker stayed with me in the hospital. Tyler evaluated the damage once they were let in and after taking some photos for insurance, has already started the cleanup process.

The last I heard, Neil was in custody. The fire chief found accelerant and grainy surveillance video of Neil walking from the restaurant in a hoodie about ten minutes before the fire. That guy flipped his rocker after getting fired. A chill works down my spine.

Hopefully, that douche is out of our lives for good. We're going to be cleaning up his mess for a while now.

Staring at Tucker's strong hands protecting mine, I know we can manage anything. But his silence is unnerving. "Tucker, talk to me."

"I don't want you to go home." My head cocks to the side, confused. His beautiful smile eases some of the worry in my chest. "I mean... I want you with me, not in that little studio apartment. I want your face beside me every night when I fall asleep and every morning when we wake up. I want to cook together, and fight together, and love together. Move in with me."

Tears blur my eyes, and I swallow. Tucker's lips pinch in a thin line, looking like he's fighting to stay quiet. Before the fire, I would have been too scared to take what I wanted, to leap without that safety net. But what the hell am I scared of? The man on the couch in front of me is honest and loyal, protective to a fault. I mean, the man ran into a burning building to save me.

Leaning forward, I know I should pay him back for that hangry comment, but all I can think of is the future. I press a gentle kiss to his lips, urging them to relax. We taste each other, our passion growing hot despite the less-than-stellar environment.

Finally, I pull back, squeezing Tucker's hand in mine. "Nothing would make me happier, boss."

He groans, rolling his eyes to the drop ceiling. "Ugh, woman! Not with the boss thing again."

I hope you've enjoyed Tucker & Bree's story.
If you did, please consider leaving a review or drop on Amazon.
com.

KEEP READING TO SEE WHAT HAPPENS AFTER THE DUST SETTLES.

Up next in the Bourbon Series is... Bourbon & Blindside by Britney Bell.

If you'd like to read where Tyler & Melanie's romance began, check here... Sunshine & Sabotage.

Epilogue

Bree

Sunshine streams across the street downtown, shining optimism across the town.

It seems everyone showed up for *Two-Fourteen's* reopening. A red ribbon stretches across the door, waiting for the massive scissors the mayor let Tucker borrow.

I snuggle deeper in my puffer jacket, burying my hands in my pockets against the October chill. I'm layered underneath this damn thing, ready to get back to work once the doors open.

Tonight is all about family, friends, and the community who supported us rebuilding. Including the lovely ladies standing on the other side of the crowd. They wave excitedly, hopping back and forth to keep warm like most of the celebrators. Lex's crew is amazing.

We only just met and yet they willingly delayed their grand opening party until they could host it with us. I mean, they already opened their doors. Lex just called it delayed gratification.

Thankfully, Tyler and Tucker repaired the fire damage fast, because I'm ready to get my ass back in the kitchen.

Speak of the devils...

Tyler and Tucker step from inside the restaurant to greet their cheering crowd. Kelsey steps up beside them, showing management's support. All the servers and kitchen crew, including two new hires, fill in the sidewalk around me.

"Get on with it!" shouts from the back and everyone laughs.

Tucker walks to the front, catching my eye with a wink before turning to address our town.

"First, I want to thank you all for showing up. I know you're cold, so I'll be quick." A chuckle works through the crowd. Everyone wiggles in their spot like worms trying to stay warm. "We wouldn't be here without all your support." A bright smile lights up his face as he claps Tyler on the back. "My nephew, Tyler. The greatest handyman and remodeler in the tri-state area. My staff." His arm sweeps by us all. "*Two-Fourteen* wouldn't be what it is without all your hard work."

"Our community showed up for us these past few weeks with your patience and your helping hands. We couldn't be more grateful."

A round of applause rolls through the crowd and the mayor steps forward, offering Tucker the giant plastic scissors. He shakes his head, and she steps back.

"There's one more person I need to thank." Tucker's hazel eyes lock on me.

"Oh, good lord. Don't."

He grins and holds out his hand. "Bree, can you come up here a minute?"

I hesitate, but a shove from Mark pushes me forward. "Hey!"

Tucker meets me halfway, grabbing my hand to tug me front and center. I swallow, wondering what the hell the man is doing.

Just cut the ribbon already, so I can get to cooking.

Tucker

Bree's deer in headlight look gives me pause.

Maybe this isn't the best idea. Bree is a very private person. I couldn't wait anymore, though.

This ring has burned a hole in my pocket for weeks. Since the day I brought her home from the hospital. I ran out to get her prescription inhaler and happened to catch a display of vintage rings in one of the shop windows. After nearly losing her over someone's grudge towards me, I knew there was no way I'd ever risk letting her go.

Now, staring into those giant green eyes, I worry that doing this in front of our entire town wasn't a great idea.

"Bree, I want you to know that I couldn't have done any of this without you." She shakes her head, but I plow through. "Okay, maybe I would have opened the restaurant, but it wouldn't have been nearly as rewarding. You've been a part of this place, a part of me, for over a year now. I've watched you make yourself completely vital to all of us. Me most of all." I wink, stroking across the blush that tints her cheeks.

"You have creativity and smarts unlike anyone I've met. It's an inspiration just to work beside you in the kitchen. You have the biggest heart, even if you keep it protected. All that does is make the lucky few of us you let in realize what gold we hold in our hands."

A lone tear slides down her cheek, and I kiss it away before dropping to a knee. The people gasp, making my heart thud harder. Her hand shakes in mine, but I hang on for dear life, praying for happily ever after with this woman.

Swallowing, I pull out the velvet box and open it to show Bree the three-carat estate emerald I pray she likes. It's large, but vintage and classy. It's got flare without being stuffy or uptight.

"Bree, if you let me hold that heart, I promise to keep it safe. All I want is you by my side as we build our future together. I was to lift each other to be stronger. I want those snuggly days off where we stay in our pajamas. And years of fighting love handles because your muffins are too damn good not to eat." The crowd snickers.

"Bree, I want everything with you. Will you be my wife?"

Silence fills the air, causing a ringing in my ear as I watch her eyes grow glassy. *Please, God.*

Finally, she nods, hiding her trembling lips behind her hand. "Yes! Yes! I would love to be your wife, Tucker."

A round of cheers screams from the crowd as I lift my fiancée in my arms, swinging her in a circle as we hold on to each other for dear life. Bree's hands lock on my face, bringing me in for a scorching kiss that has me grinning against her mouth.

"Get it, boy!" shouts one of the little old ladies in the crowd.

My face heats, but I let Bree slide down my front, hiding my erection in the front of her coat, so I can slide my ring on her finger.

"If you'd rather have a diamond, I completely understand. This one matched your eyes, but we can get you whatever you want." I grip her chin and stare into the most beautiful face on this green Earth, so thankful that I'm the lucky bastard that gets to hold her.

"Now, what do you say we open our restaurant, my love?"

Grinning, she accepts the scissors from the mayor and passes me one side. "Here's to the future, Bossman."

Growling, I lean in and nip her ear. "Save that for later, sassy pants." And with that, we cut the path to our future and spend the next thirty minutes accepting well wishes before making it to the kitchen where it all began.

PLEASE DON'T FORGET TO LEAVE A REVIEW <3
Bourbon & Boss

Next UP... Bourbon & Blindsideby Britney Bell

**Pre-ORDER now... WELCOME TO KISSING SPRINGS...
MIDNIGHT SEASON**

Midnight & Mistakes

Kelsey:

Being a mom is my life. Work. Home. Work. Home.

I wasn't all that keen on a vacation when the people in my life shoved me into taking a break. However, one breath of fresh mountain air, that first view of fresh powder, renew the fire missing in my life...

Maybe allowing myself a little taste of mountain man candy could put the icing on my little forced getaway.

Ace:

I'm not great at a lot, but my spot on this mountain is fixed. My career as a Medic in the army combined with my love of the slopes and isolation creates a perfect hybrid for the carefree bachelor life. When duty calls, it's status quo, just another day on the job, until one stubborn blonde turns my carefully detached bedside manner on its head. She's a ball of fire inside a delicate shell, beautiful and fragile, prickly perfection.

Our lives don't work. She's injured, vulnerable. I should just mend her and let her go. Too bad my brain and my heart have other ideas.

Also By Annie

BIG PAW MOUNTAIN SERIES

Shattered Illusions: A Bear Shifter Paranormal
Romance

Beyond Expectations: A Bear Shifter +
Firefighter Paranormal Romance ← Sign up for preview & get
notified on release day!

DIXON DRAGON MAFIA

Unleashed: Dixon's Dragon Mafia

WELCOME TO KISSING SPRINGS

Salty Santa – *Also, available in German.*

Sunshine & Sabotage– *Also, available in German.*

Bourbon Boss

FOLLOW ON **REAM STORIES!**

Follow The Kissing Springs Book Babes

Join us in our Facebook group, celebrating all things about the
small town of Kissing
Springs, and our steamy book series.
We share recipes, cocktails, tips, freebies, cover reveals, author in-
sights, and more fun.
Go to: Welcome to Kissing Springs Reader Group on Facebook.
Sign up for monthly news and updates:
www.kissingsprings.com/welcome

The Welcome to Kissing Springs Series

Santa Season:

Single Santa, by Zee Irwin

Secret Santa, by Kristin Lee

Silver Santa, by Joi Jackson

Salty Santa, by Annie Rae

Scoring Santa, by Britney Bell

Shameless Santa, by Tracy Broemmer

Snappy Santa, by Grace Grahme

Scorching Santa, by Ellen Brooks

Sunshine Season:

Sunshine and Secrets, by Zee Irwin

Sunshine and Saddles, by Kristin Lee

Sunshine and Silk Boxers, by Joi Jackson

Sunshine and Sabotage, by Annie Rae

Sunshine and Sidelines, by Britney Bell

Sunshine and Soulmates, by Tracy Broemmer

Sunshine and Scandals, by Grace Grahme

Sunshine and Sass, by Ellen Brooks

Coming Soon:

Welcome to Kissing Springs: Bourbon Season, Fall 2023

About the Author

Annie Rae

Annie is a wife and mom, living in Texas with her two amazing kiddos, dogs, bunnies, and the sexiest, suited, mountain-man a girl could dream to be her prince (beard included).

Weekends are for cheering on the kiddos in all their craziness and curling up with a steamy romance book and missing too much sleep because of it. The self-proclaimed sunflower would love nothing more than to be on a beach, writing her day away.

Annie loves escaping into great novels where you ride the ride and feel the emotions of great characters, laughing with them, crying with them, and missing them after "the end." It is a dream come true to be able to write about those protective heroes, fated love, and happy endings.

Follow Annie for more fabulous book boyfriends and playful laughs.

www.AuthorAnnieRae.com